TENDER LOVE

A CHRISTIAN ROMANCE

JULIETTE DUNCAN

BOOK 1 "THE TRUE LOVE SERIES"

COPYRIGHT

PRAISE FOR "TENDER LOVE"

"Really enjoyed reading this book. Appreciated the mixed family, divorce healing, true to life in these days, narrative. Appreciate clean dialog, but best of all just that it was interesting and made me want to keep reading. Always like books that inspire my faith." *Reader*

"Love this book! I hated for it to end. If you love a good clean romance novel, you'll love this book!" *K McKinley*

"Very interesting and a real page turner. Couldn't put it down. Great reading a good clean Christian love story." *CA Cookie*

"A very beautiful book, love is a choice guided and directed by the author of love Himself, God Almighty and courtship is still a way of life." *Reader*

ALSO BY JULIETTE DUNCAN

Contemporary Christian Romance
The Shadows Series
Lingering Shadows
Facing the Shadows
Beyond the Shadows
Secrets and Sacrifice
A Highland Christmas

The True Love Series
Tender Love
Tested Love
Tormented Love
Triumphant Love
True Love at Christmas
Promises of Love

Precious Love Series
Forever Cherished
Forever Faithful (coming early 2018)

Middle Grade Christian Fiction
The Madeleine Richards Series

CHAPTER 1

$\mathcal{B}$risbane, Australia

EARLY MORNING SUNSHINE streamed through the white lace curtains of Tessa Scott's pocket-sized bedroom, but inside her heart, it rained. Nearly three months had passed since she had formally ended her relationship with Michael Urbane, and although she firmly believed it had been the right thing to do, pain still squeezed her heart whenever she thought of him.

Some days were easier than others, but the past two days had been especially hard. Yesterday had been Michael's birthday. How tempted she'd been to call him and at least wish him 'happy birthday'. Last year she'd surprised him with a day trip snorkelling on Moreton Island. They'd had so much fun—they always did, and the very memory of that wonderfully happy, sun-filled day only made it worse. She shouldn't let her mind go there, but she couldn't help it, and images of their day snorkelling amongst the coral and the myriads of brightly coloured fish played over and over in her mind.

Burying her head in her pillow, Tessa sobbed silent tears. It hurt so badly. If only the accident at his work hadn't happened. *Or he hadn't lied about the drugs.* She inhaled deeply as a sob escaped, sending another wave of sadness through her body. *Why couldn't she let go?* Maybe she should give him another chance? *But it would never be the same.* She knew that. Their adventure had died, and she needed to accept it.

A soft knock on the door interrupted her thoughts. The gentle but firm voice of her housemate, Stephanie, sounded on the other side. "Tess, you need to get up."

Tessa buried her head deeper in the pillows.

The door creaked open and Stephanie tip-toed in, placing a cup of spiced chai tea on Tessa's nightstand. The aromatic mixture of cardamom, cinnamon, ginger and other herbs filled the room, tickling her nose. Steph knew the trick to getting her up.

She gave in and raised her head. "What time is it?"

"Time to get up, that's what." Dressed in a smart business suit, Stephanie placed her hands on her hips and studied Tessa with an air of disapproval. "Don't tell me you've been crying over Michael again?"

Tessa sat up and took a sip of tea before meeting her friend's gaze. "Just thinking about him, that's all."

Stephanie shook her head and let out a frustrated sigh. "I know you're grieving, but it's been months since you broke up. Come on. Get out of bed and get ready for work. Your boss called and said she'd place you on unpaid leave if you call in sick one more time. I was tempted to tell her you weren't even sick."

"But I have been sick." Tessa leaned back against her bedhead and bit her lip, forcing herself not to cry in front of Stephanie.

"I know." Sitting on the edge of the bed, Stephanie took hold of Tessa's free hand. "It's hard to let go, especially having been together for so long. But breaking up was the only option. You know that."

"But maybe I was too hard on him." Tessa grabbed a tissue and wiped her eyes. "Those drugs changed him, Steph. He wasn't himself."

"I know. But you did try to help him. For months. I watched you slowly being torn apart. The truth is, you can't help someone who doesn't want to be helped." Stephanie squeezed her hand. "You can't help someone who lies to you about their addiction, even if it is to prescription drugs. *And he stole from you.* You need honesty in your relationship, and Michael wasn't willing to give that to you. You did the right thing. You're better off without him."

"It's just hard not knowing where he is or how he's doing." Tessa glanced at the photo of him still sitting on her dresser. "It's hard being single again. I feel …" She paused and searched for the right word, as the ache in her chest grew. "Lonely."

"You poor thing." Stephanie leaned forward and hugged her tightly. "I'm here for you, Tess. And so's God, you know that. I understand you feel bad about this whole situation, but God's with you, and He'll help you through it. And you never know what, or who, He might have in store for you!" She gently brushed the stray hair from Tessa's face and gave her another hug.

Tessa nodded reluctantly. Steph was right. She'd made the right decision and knew that God would be with her and would help her through it, but translating that knowledge to her heart was another matter altogether.

"Come on kiddo, breakfast's ready. Let's get you up, dressed, and off to work."

TESSA SLID out of bed as Stephanie retreated to the kitchen. As she swallowed down the rest of her tea, Michael's photo caught her attention once again. Grey eyes with a hint of blue in a tanned, chiselled face stared out at her, tugging at her heart-strings. She picked up the photo and flopped back onto her bed, gazing at the face that was so familiar. This torture had to end. She traced the outline of his face with her finger before hugging the photo to her chest. Closing her eyes, she squeezed back hot tears. This was it. The end.

"God, please help me get through this day." Her body shuddered as she gulped down unbidden sobs. *"I'm sorry it's taken so long, but I'm ready to let go. Please help me."* Tears streamed down her face as she hugged the photo tightly one last time before she opened the bottom drawer of her dresser and stuffed the photo under the pile of chunky knit sweaters she rarely wore.

Time to move on, and with God's help, she would.

CHAPTER 2

a short while later, Tessa paused and took a deep breath before poking her head into her boss's office. She should have been more communicative with Fran rather than just providing lame excuses for not being at work for the past two weeks. Too late now. Hopefully she'd be understanding.

Fran, a petite, hazel-eyed ginger, replaced the receiver and looked up in surprise at Tessa. "Good to see you back at last, Tessa. Come in. Are you better?"

"Yes, thank you." Tessa smiled gratefully at her boss, who, without any more ado, picked up a chart from her desk and handed it to her. *Straight back into it...* Tessa laughed to herself at the brusque, business-like manner Fran put on whenever she wanted to show who was boss.

"A rabbit, a bull terrier, and a cat all need surgery this morning, so I'm glad you're back. Not sure the new girl could handle three operations in a row." Fran peered over the top of her funky green rimmed glasses. "What's that you're carrying?"

Tessa looked down at the skinny, shivering puppy tucked under her arm. How could she have forgotten about him? "Poor little thing. Nearly ran him over in the parking lot. Must have been dumped." She lifted him up. "Only about three months old. How could anyone not want him?"

The puppy's sad little eyes pleaded with hers. She pulled him close and hugged him.

Fran shook her head and sighed with exasperation. "We get too many of these. You know that."

"I'll clean him up, and if no one claims him, I might just keep this one." Tessa stroked the puppy's little head and gave a small laugh as he licked her face.

"Well, that's your decision. but now, off with you. There's plenty to do." Fran waved her out of the office, and despite her brusque manner, her face had softened into a friendly grin.

Tessa finished operating on the three animals just before lunch. Later in the day she returned the pets to their owners with several pieces of post-surgery advice. The relief on each of their faces warmed her heart and reminded her just how much she loved this work.

At the end of the day as she headed for the door, Fran called out. "Cathy and I are going for burgers. Would you like to join us?"

"No, but thanks for asking. I'm going to take this little puppy home and clean him up properly."

Fran gave the pup a tickle behind his ears. "He is a cute one, I'll give him that." She looked over her glasses. "It's good to have you back, Tess."

"Thanks. It's good to be back." Tessa's voice faltered slightly as she gave her boss a grateful smile.

As she headed for her sky-blue Hatchback in the parking lot across the street from the veterinary clinic, she had a new spring to her step. Yes, it *was* good to be back. Today had gone better than expected. Michael hadn't come to her mind once, and she'd even gained a new friend. Why hadn't she come back sooner?

Humming along to the praise music coming from the car radio, she drummed her fingers on the steering wheel and glanced at the puppy in the passenger seat. Despite her intentions, she hadn't had time to clean him at the clinic. His fur, matted and dirty, should clean to a reddish brown. He seemed more relaxed now as he tugged and chewed at the towel she'd placed on the seat, and she laughed at his antics.

"What are we going to call you? Let's see... Samson?" She studied him carefully as she sat at a red light. "No, you're not big enough for a name like that. Shadow? No. How about Sammy?" *Why are all my names starting with an 's'?* The lights changed and she accelerated quickly to keep up with the traffic. She glanced at him again. "Sparky? Yes, that's it. Sparky suits you perfectly."

She laughed as the puppy gave a short, sharp bark as if voicing his agreement.

Arriving at the small, recently renovated worker's cottage she shared with Stephanie, she changed out of her work clothes and found an old basin. She filled it with warm, soapy water and proceeded to clean the pup. She was drying him when Stephanie returned.

"Where are you, Tess?" The thud of Stephanie's briefcase landing on the kitchen table reached the bathroom.

"Bathroom. Come and look."

Stephanie took the few steps from the kitchen and stopped in the doorway, her jaw dropping. "A dog! What's a dog doing in our bathroom?"

"He's only a puppy. I found him this morning in the parking lot and hoped you wouldn't mind." Tessa gave the pup another rub and lifted him up. "I named him Sparky. He's so cute. Look at him."

But Stephanie wasn't amused.

"Don't worry about dinner, I ordered Chinese takeout."

Stephanie shook her head and rolled her eyes. "Whatever." She let out a resigned sigh. "Hope it won't be long, I'm starving." Collapsing on the couch, she kicked off her shoes. Sparky immediately made a dash for them, dragging one across the hardwood floor. She pulled it out of his mouth before turning her attention back to Tessa. "Did Fran chew you out?"

"No. Everyone was happy to see me, and I actually had a great day." Tessa picked Sparky up and sat down beside Stephanie. "You were right. I should've gone back earlier." She patted Sparky on the head as he tried to lick her hand. "How did your day go?"

"Had a pop quiz this morning at college. Piece of cake." Stephanie sat up and pulled some brightly coloured files from her brief case and flicked through them. "But this afternoon at work…" She sighed heavily and slumped back on the couch.

"What's up?"

"Oh, I don't know. Guess I'm just starting to question whether I'm cut out for this type of work or not. I got assigned some new cases last week. One's a teenage girl whose mother's an alcoholic. She's got a younger brother, and they're both in and out of foster care. I'm supposed to check on them every day. *Every day!* I feel so sorry for them, but I don't know what I can do to help them. They're really messed up, and their current foster family has just about had enough."

"It can't be that bad. You're so good at sorting out problems." Tessa squeezed her hand. "You'll be able to do something. I know you will."

Stephanie shrugged wearily. "And there's this other lady, Gwen. She's terrified of getting cancer. I understand her concern a little because one of her aunts and her only sister died of ovarian cancer, and just last month her mum died from breast cancer." She looked up, her eyes heavy with concern.

"Now she wants to have a preventive double mastectomy and have her ovaries removed. The problem is, her husband doesn't want her to, and they're arguing about it. They were referred to the centre to try to resolve their differences, but I'm at a loss as to how to help. It's likely their marriage will break up soon if we can't help them reach a resolution."

"Can you discuss it with your manager? Surely he can help." Tessa hated seeing her best friend so torn up about her work. Steph's problem was that she cared too much.

Stephanie let out a dejected sigh. "I guess so. But he'll think I'm useless if I do."

"Surely not. It's a Christian Counselling Centre, for goodness sake. They should be supporting you as much as they can, especially while you're still in training."

"You'd think so, but they're tough on newbies."

Tessa glanced at the files, each bearing a bold red *Confiden-*

tial stamp. They shouldn't be discussing these cases. *Her patients were different.* Chatting about the animals she operated on would never get her in hot water, but Steph's patients were people, and she could get into big trouble if she got caught talking about them with anyone outside the centre.

She'd get defensive, but Tessa had to bring it up. Sparky wriggled and she placed him on the floor. She hated confronting Steph like this, but she had no choice. She turned around and sat square on, facing her as she tucked one leg under the other.

"Steph, should you be talking to me about your cases? I'd hate you to get into trouble."

Stephanie fidgeted with her hands, but held Tessa's gaze for a moment before lowering her eyes. "Probably not, but I have to talk to someone or I'll go crazy." She looked up, her eyes glistening.

Tessa's voice softened. "It's really getting to you, isn't it?"

Stephanie nodded and turned her head away.

"Let me make you a cup of tea." Tessa squeezed her friend's shoulder before hopping off the couch.

"Thanks." Steph pulled a tissue from the box on the side table and blew her nose. "This is really stupid. I'm sorry."

"Would you like to pray about it?"

She nodded. Her body shuddered as she sucked in a big breath.

Tessa sat back down again, and placing an arm around her shoulder, bowed her head. "Lord God, I pray for Stephanie right now. You know she has a heart for people who are hurting and that she really wants to help them, so please give her wisdom and confidence when she meets with them, especially with those she's mentioned just now. Let your love shine through her to them, and Lord, please work in each of their lives and give them a sense of hope that their problems might have a resolution. Thank you for Stephanie's commitment to do your work and for her love and compassion for others. I pray that you'll meet her needs, Lord God, and help her in all she does. In Jesus' precious name, Amen."

She gave Stephanie a big hug, holding her tight.

Tears streamed down Stephanie's cheeks. She sniffed and gave Tessa a watery smile as she dabbed her face with a tissue. "Thanks. I don't know what I'd do without you."

"You'd survive, Stephanie Trejo. You're the strong one, remember?" Tessa gave her another hug as a knock sounded on their door.

"That must be dinner. Good timing!" Tessa stood and reached the front door in two strides.

Stephanie continued talking about her work as they ate, like she needed to get it off her chest although now she was more composed. Tessa wasn't completely happy about listening, but what else could she do after all the nonsense she'd put Stephanie through after her breakup with Michael? Steph had been so patient and had helped her so much, the least she could do was listen, but as Steph told her about yet another case, she hoped and prayed she'd never run into any of these people at the store or café in town.

"This guy's wife divorced him after running off with another man and leaving him to raise their teenage son on his own. I'm sure he's suffering from depression, but he refuses to talk about it and instead gives me a hard time at every meeting. I don't even know why he comes." Stephanie sighed and rested her chin in her hands. "I have absolutely no idea how to get through to him." She looked up, exhaling slowly. Her eyes had watered once again. "I have to do case studies on them all, and I don't even know where to begin, especially with Mr. Williams. He's so stiff, we don't even use first names."

Tessa squeezed her hand. "I'm sure God will help you find a way. Hang in there, Steph."

CHAPTER 3

"*N*o!" Stephanie gasped as she opened the front door of their cottage a few days later. Tessa hurried up the steps and her heart fell as she peered around Stephanie at the mess. Stepping carefully over a lamp on the floor, she set the load of shopping bags in her arms onto the nearby table. A couple of cushions had been torn open and stuffing covered the floor. Another lamp had been knocked from the living room coffee table, several pairs of shoes from Stephanie's closet lay in the hallway, and bathroom tissue littered the entire house.

"What a mess! Sparky, where are you?" Raising her voice, she strode into the kitchen. The pup emerged from under the table tangled in tissue, his soft brown eyes imploring her not to be angry.

"You're such a naughty boy!" She grabbed him and pulled the paper off him. "It's not going to work on me." But when he licked her face with his wet, pink tongue, she couldn't help herself and burst out laughing.

"I don't see what's funny." Stephanie stood in the doorway waving a pair of dark blue ballet flats in Tessa's direction. "That troublemaker of yours has ripped up my favourite shoes."

"He just needs to be trained, Steph. I'm sorry. I'll buy you a new pair." Tessa hugged the puppy closer and planted a kiss on top of his head. "Cathy's husband has just started his own dog and puppy training courses. I'll sign up for classes."

"Good idea." Stephanie huffed as she inspected her destroyed shoes.

"I'll clean up the mess and then fix us a nice lunch. I'm really sorry, Steph. Truly I am."

Stephanie huffed again as she walked back to her room, but Tessa knew she didn't mean it.

Half an hour later, with the house tidied, the two girls sat down to rounds of toasted ham, cheese and tomato sandwiches. Sparky was back in his pen and Tessa laughed at the pitiful look on his face.

"He may be a troublemaker, but at least one good thing has come out of having him here."

Tessa looked up. This was a surprise coming from Stephanie. "What's that?"

"He's kept your mind off Michael. You've stopped moping about him."

"True." She'd hardly thought about him since bringing Sparky home. A pang of guilt hit her. How was it possible to completely let go of someone who'd been such a major part of your life for so long? And so quickly? Was she a bad person to have done that? Surely not, but still, it didn't seem right to have forgotten about him completely. Maybe she should check on him.

"A dog might be helpful for that man I told you about the other night. You know, the one whose wife walked out on him?" Stephanie placed her knife neatly on her plate. Tessa nodded her head slowly, struggling to remember which one Steph was referring to. She'd mentioned so many.

"Think I'll suggest it to him. Might help with his depression."

"Oh, that one. Yes, a dog might help, but make sure he wants one first. I see too many unwanted animals in my line of work. And pets can't fix everything."

She looked at Sparky and her heart warmed. Getting a dog had certainly helped her—who was she to deny anyone else that opportunity?

"No, but it might be part of the solution. I'll suggest it at our next meeting." Stephanie shrugged. "He doesn't have to take my advice."

Tessa collected the dirty plates and carried them to the kitchen. She didn't want to debate the merits or otherwise of having a pet right now. But yes, a dog could help the guy. And at least it might help Stephanie feel like she was doing something.

The phone rang just as Tessa started the dishes. She dried her hands and answered it. Her brother, Elliott, was on the line.

"Hey, sis." She smiled to herself. It was so good to hear his voice. "I'm back from the States and it'd be good to catch up. I assume you've remembered it's Mum and Dad's thirtieth wedding anniversary in a few weeks?"

"Yes…" *No…* She'd actually forgotten about her parents' anniversary, but she wasn't about to admit that to her younger brother.

"We need to discuss what we're doing for them. They've stepped out to run some errands, so now's a good time for you to come over if you've got a few minutes."

She shook her head and laughed.

"You haven't changed, Elliott. I'll be there shortly."

WHEN TESSA ARRIVED SOON AFTER, Elliott was outside on their parents' driveway polishing his motorcycle under the shade of a magnificent frangipani tree.

"See you've got a new friend there, sis. Better let him out." He nodded towards Sparky, who was scratching at the car window. Elliott stopped polishing his bike and gave her a bear hug before she opened the door and let the pup out.

Elliott bent down and patted him before leaning against his bike and folding his arms. "So, how have you been doing, sis?"

For a moment, she was tempted to tell him about her recent heartache over Michael. But he probably already knew they'd broken up—Mum would have told him. Elliott had never much liked Michael, anyway. No, she wouldn't mention the breakup unless he did.

"I'm doing all right. And you?" She picked Sparky up to stop him jumping on Elliott. *The sooner I can start those lessons the better.*

"I can't complain. Next month I go on my first official

mission trip to Ecuador. Finally get to put all that theory into practice. Can't wait."

She smiled at her brother's enthusiasm for sharing Christ with peoples in other cultures. He'd always been the adventurer of the family, and he had such a zeal to serve God.

"Now, regarding our parents' anniversary," she said, trying to hold Sparky still. "I was thinking something simple. Maybe just a family dinner someplace special."

"They go to dinner all the time. Come on, sis. Not every couple reaches their Pearl wedding anniversary. This needs to be extravagant." His eyes lit up. "I'm thinking a catered, candle-light dinner at a beach-side restaurant, followed by a night in a hotel, and then a whale watching cruise. What do you think?"

Tessa shook her head and laughed. How did he come up with ideas like this? Maybe he was right, but her parents were quiet and conservative. What if they didn't appreciate all the fuss? "Mum would love the cruise. She's always wanted to go on one. So, I guess… I just hope they like it."

Elliott beamed, his deep blue eyes standing out in his paler than normal skin. "Great. We could invite all their friends from work and church, and Pastor Stanek, of course."

"It sounds great."

"I'll sort the details, but sis, you take care of the guest list. Whatever you do, remember this is a surprise, so don't say a word about it to them."

"My lips are sealed." Tessa grinned fondly at her gregarious little brother as they shook the special handshake they'd created as children for keeping secrets.

As she drove away, excitement about the plans they'd just made for her parents grew. It would be a special celebration for them, and she couldn't wait to see their faces when they arrived at the restaurant and found out about the night in the hotel and the cruise. She hoped they'd enjoy it. Thirty years of marriage hadn't always been easy for her parents but it was an achievement worthy of celebration.

Would she ever find someone to spend three decades with? At one time she'd thought it would have been with Michael, but now? A lone tear escaped from the corner of her eye and rolled down her cheek. She wiped it away with the back of her hand as she pulled into her driveway. She and Michael had always done such fun things together. In fact, their whole relationship had been built on having fun. He was such a big kid. Who would she have fun with now that Michael was no longer around?

Not Steph—she was so serious of late. And not Mum and Dad. They were so straight and conservative. It had always been her and Michael. At least Elliott would be around for a while, but then he'd be off again on one of his adventures. Tessa's eyes blurred with tears as the old familiar ache found its way back to her heart.

CHAPTER 4

*J*essa pulled up outside Cathy's large ranch-style house for Sparky's first puppy training class the following Thursday evening. The number of cars already parked under the large gum trees surprised her; it seemed Cathy's husband, Dave, had already developed a good reputation. It had taken more than half an hour to drive from New Farm to the leafy suburb of Ferny Hills in the west of the city, and she'd only just made it. The traffic had been a nightmare and she'd started to think a closer one would have been smarter.

She turned off the engine and picked up Sparky's leash. "Well, young man, this is it. Time to grow up and learn to behave." She ruffled his head and chuckled at his eagerness to lick her at every opportunity.

No need for the signs pointing towards the garage that Dave had turned into a canine training school. The noise of yapping dogs reached her ears long before she reached it. Dogs of all shapes, sizes, and breeds filled the various areas inside the building. She leaned close to hear the assistant's directions to the puppy class about to start outside. Dave welcomed her as she joined the group.

"Sorry I'm late." She flashed an apologetic smile and pulled Sparky into line as best she could. Cathy had told her Dave used to be a shearer. His bulging arms suggested he must still work out.

"No problem. Welcome." He offered a short smile and lifted his cap before returning his attention to the group. "Now you're all here, take a few moments to introduce yourselves to each other before we begin the class. I'd like to see how the pups interact with each other, so let them off their leashes if you feel comfortable." His sun hardened face crinkled into an infectious grin. "Don't worry. They can't escape—it's all fenced."

Tessa bent down and unclipped Sparky's leash before shaking hands with the dark-haired woman standing beside her. They both laughed as Sparky darted back and forth across the grass, sniffing at everything and everyone in his path.

"Looks like you've got the most active pup of the bunch." Although deep, the voice behind her was friendly, warm, *and mesmerising*.

Tessa turned around slowly. Before her stood a slim, attractive man with short, dark brown hair and milk chocolate eyes, dressed in a smart white polo shirt, cargo shorts and Nike joggers. Her heart skipped a beat and for once she struggled for words.

"My pup's quite shy, unlike yours." The man bent down to

pat Sparky, who'd returned to check on Tessa and yapped excitedly as he spun around in circles.

"Yes, he never stops." She glanced around for the man's dog and let out a nervous laugh. He pointed to the fence where a teenage boy stood holding a black terrier pup.

"Your son? He looks like you." *Why did I say that? I can hardly see the boy's face under his hair...*

"Yes, my son Jayden. And I'm Ben... Ben Williams." The man hesitated, but then extended his hand. Her eyes widened. *Ben Williams? No! It can't be Stephanie's depressed patient, surely? Or could it?* Her heart pounded. *What am I going to do?*

If it *was* him, no way could she let slip she knew bits and pieces about him, *or that her best friend happened to be his counsellor.* He stared at her curiously, his hand still outstretched.

"Are you all right? Has something happened?"

"Ah, yes. I'm fine." She controlled herself and shook his hand—perhaps a little too vigorously. "I'm Tessa. Tessa Scott, but just call me Tess if you want. Most people do." She was talking way too much.

"Nice to meet you, Tess."

Her cheeks warmed under his gaze. How could this personable man before her give anyone, least of all Stephanie, a hard time? Standing a head taller than her, his slim body was toned, but not as muscly as Michael's. His eyes held a tinge of sadness, but she certainly wouldn't call them depressed. She made a mental note to reprimand Stephanie for needlessly exaggerating Ben Williams' state of mind.

His smooth deep voice brought her back to the moment when he introduced his son, Jayden. The boy's hair was the same colour as his father's, but his head hung low, and under his baseball cap, she had no idea if his eyes were the same as Ben's or not. Only when she asked for the dog's name did he look up. Yes, the same eyes, although they were hard, unlike his father's.

"It's Bindy. She's a Scottish Terrier." Jayden pulled the dog closer to his chest, but wore a sullen look on his face, as if he'd only come under sufferance.

She was just about to respond when Dave called everyone to attention and began the first lesson. With the noise from the other trainers and dogs, Tessa had trouble getting Sparky to listen to her, especially as he seemed more interested in what the other dogs were doing.

She couldn't help but watch Jayden and Ben out of the corner of her eye as they worked with Bindy. Jayden became animated as he interacted with the pup. His face even lit up a little every time Bindy responded to one of his commands. And Ben was very encouraging with Jayden. Not how Stephanie described him at all.

As everyone began to leave, she stepped in beside Jayden. The boy was obviously having a difficult time, and her heart went out to him.

"Hey Jayden, I was impressed with the way you handled Bindy tonight. Better than me with Sparky." She let out a small laugh as he shot her a suspicious look, but when she stopped and patted Bindy, a faint smile showed on his face.

"What do you say to the lady, Jayden?"

Jayden rolled his eyes. "Thank you." He glanced up but lowered his gaze quickly.

Tessa chuckled, but wondered why teenagers had to be so difficult.

When they reached the car park, Ben slowed. "Why don't you take both dogs for a short walk, Jayden?" He turned to her. "As long as that's okay with you?"

Her heart quickened as his eyes met hers. What was happening? What was the look she'd seen? Had she really seen something, or was it just her overactive imagination? Or was it just wishful thinking? *Take a grip, Tessa. You've only just met the man, and he has a teenage son. Don't even go there.* "Yes, that's fine." She forced herself to respond normally, trying not to let any of her crazy thoughts show in her voice.

"I'll admit I wasn't that keen about getting a pet," he said quietly once Jayden had moved out of hearing range. "Seems to be helping, though. With him." Ben nodded towards his son and let out a heavy sigh.

"Teenagers aren't the easiest of people. I remember what I was like. And my brother Elliott, he was even worse." Tessa shoved her hands into her pockets and let out a small laugh. Her heart beat so loudly she hoped he couldn't hear it.

"Don't I know. My counsellor suggested we get a dog. Thought it might help improve our..." He paused, as if searching for the right word. "Relationship."

"You're getting counselling?" Tessa gritted her teeth and berated herself for yet again speaking before thinking. *Why did I ask that? Stupid. Stupid.*

She held her breath. He took a long time to answer, his shoulders drooping as he let out a resigned sigh.

"Yes. Just trying to work through some personal issues."

Don't ask. Don't ask... She steeled herself and considered her reply. "Dogs can be miracle workers. Sparky's helped improve my outlook on life already, and I've only had him a couple of weeks." *That's better. Keep it neutral.*

He leaned on his car, a fancy looking thing, and looked wistfully at Jayden. *If only he'd smile. Maybe Steph was right and he is depressed.* She felt like giving him a big hug and telling him it was all right, but that certainly would be acting rashly. She barely knew the man.

"I think I'd say the same for Jayden. We've only had Bindy a couple of days, but she seems to have made a real difference to him already."

"That's wonderful." Her pulse quickened as he turned his gaze towards her. Was it her imagination again, or was there a connection between them? She held his gaze for a moment longer before lowering her eyes. She could really embarrass herself if she wasn't careful.

"Come on, Jayden. Time to go." Ben's deep voice carried easily. He unlocked the car and held the back door open. Jayden placed Bindy on the back seat before slumping into the front passenger seat and turning on the radio.

"It's been nice meeting you, Tess. I'll look forward to seeing you next week." Ben held out his hand.

She didn't hesitate. The touch of his warm skin on hers sent tingles through her body. "I'll look forward to it too."

SHE SMILED ALL the way home. When Stephanie arrived home from work, Tessa couldn't stop gushing about Ben Williams.

"We must be talking about a different person. The Ben Williams I know doesn't say more than two words."

CHAPTER 5

essa fell asleep with Ben on her mind. When she woke, he was still on it. It was late morning, and since no surgeries were scheduled at the vet clinic, she had no need to go into work until after lunch. Stephanie had already left for college.

Had something really happened last night or had she just imagined it? He was an attractive man, no doubt about it, and her heart had pounded like that of a star-struck schoolgirl the entire time she'd been near him. He was older than any man she'd dated. Maybe that was it. He was definitely more mature than Michael, but that wouldn't be hard. Ben seemed to be a *gentleman*, not a fun loving, irresponsible twenty something.

She sat with a start and blinked. What *was* she thinking? It was silly. She knew nothing about the man. He probably wasn't even a believer. She hung her head and closed her eyes, but the image of him leaning against his car wouldn't leave her mind.

Finally, she reached for the well-worn, dog-eared Bible her

mother had given her when she turned fifteen. She normally used a Bible reading plan, but today she opened to a random place and read the first verses her eyes settled on, verses from Psalm 119: *"Blessed are those who keep his statutes and seek him with all their heart—they do no wrong but follow his ways. You have laid down precepts that are to be fully obeyed. Oh that my ways were steadfast in obeying your decrees!"*

She allowed the words to sink into her heart and mind, and after a short while bowed her head. *"Dear God, I'm sorry for acting so immaturely last night. I want to follow You with all my heart. You know that."* Clasping her hands together, she took a slow, deep breath as she rested in God's presence. Having committed her life to God when young, she knew the importance of seeking His guidance and wisdom. She wanted to do what was right in His sight, but so often she made rash decisions and was sure she let Him down. *"Lord, I can't help wondering if You brought Ben and me together, or if it was just a coincidence? Will You give me direction? Until then, I promise I won't give him another thought. Thank you. In Jesus' precious name, Amen."*

BEN STEPPED into the glass-enclosed elevator of the Elizabeth Macarthur building and waited for the lift to take him from the lobby to the fourth floor. Usually he was impatient, but not today. His mind was on Tessa Scott. He'd hardly stopped thinking about her alluring smile and happy demeanour since meeting her at the puppy training class. The way her light brown hair bounced on her shoulders and her cornflower blue eyes always seemed to be smiling were etched on his mind. Not since Kathryn had left had he felt this way about another woman. Maybe at last he was moving on.

The elevator doors opened. He exited and took a left turn down the hallway to the counsellor's office. The nameplate on the office door read *Stephanie J. Trejo, Interim Social Worker.* When he knocked, her familiar friendly voice called for him to enter.

"Mr. Williams. How are you?" Stephanie stood and shook his hand.

He grinned sheepishly. "I'm good, thanks."

Her eyes widened. "That's a first. But I have to say I'm pleased to hear it." She directed him to the armchair opposite her desk. "What's brought on the change?" She quickly shifted some magazines off the other armchair and took a seat.

"I took your suggestion and bought a dog." He paused, studying the young woman before him. He was seeing her because his doctor had suggested he talk to someone about his breakup and had referred him to this centre. Never in his wildest dreams had he thought he'd be assigned to a young intern, and a female at that.

He didn't enjoy the sessions and hadn't really warmed to her. How could a young woman like her be able to offer him any advice? She'd probably never had any real problems herself, and wouldn't have a clue about what he'd been through or was still going through. He'd been tempted to ask for someone else, and maybe he would, although she seemed professional enough. For now, he'd let her continue with explaining the various stages of grief she believed he was going through, but if he had to open up with someone, an older male would be preferable. Someone who'd seen a bit more of life. *But maybe he wouldn't need to come much longer...* Strange how comfortable he'd felt last night talking with Tessa. But that was different. She wasn't his counsellor.

Stephanie's face lit up. "A dog! That's great! What did you get?"

"A Scottish Terrier. Pure bred."

"What does your son think?"

"He loves her. It's only been a few days, but instead of watching television after school, he's coming home and playing with her. If I get home early enough, we go to the park and walk her."

"Seems like having a dog is paying off already. And if you're going to the park with your son, that's progress. But what about you? How are you feeling?"

Ben steadied his gaze on the woman. Normally he'd guard his feelings, but something had happened last night when he'd met Tessa and he had a real desire to share it with someone. But talking about it would make it real. Was he ready to take the step from fantasy to reality? He'd probably got it all wrong but steeled himself anyway and took a deep breath. "I'm good. We took Bindy to her first training class last night."

"Really? And how did that go?"

"It was... *good.* I think Jayden enjoyed it too."

"Was that a smile?"

He averted his gaze and tried to remove the grin he knew was inching up his face. "Maybe."

"Come on, Mr. Williams. What happened at dog training?"

He let out a small chuckle and shook his head. *What am I doing? I probably read too much into Tessa's friendliness. Got it all wrong.* "Nothing. The trainer's very good, and Jayden can't wait to go back. That's a real plus."

"There's more to it than that, I'm sure. Come on, tell me." Leaning back in her chair, Stephanie tapped her pencil as she studied him.

He let out another chuckle. He couldn't believe it. *How did I get myself into this?* He ran his hand through his hair and met her gaze. Although the air conditioning was on and the room's temperature was pleasant, his palms were clammy. "I guess I may as well tell you." He shrugged defensively, all the while holding her gaze. "I got talking to a young lady, that's all. She was very friendly—she even spoke with Jayden."

"I guess that explains why you're in a better mood today. Do you plan on asking her out?"

"Come on, I only just met her." But as stupid as it sounded, the thought hadn't left his mind. But he wasn't telling *her* that. He shifted in the chair and crossed his arms. "No. I don't. Not yet, anyway."

"It sounds promising, though." Stephanie smiled, an expression he couldn't pick flashing across her face.

Ben shrugged without enthusiasm, trying to play down how he really felt. "We'll see. We only just met. And besides, I don't know if I want to get involved with anyone after how things ended with Kathryn." And that was the truth. Kathryn's sudden leaving more than a year and a half ago had thrown him so much he felt anything but confident when it came to relationships.

Stephanie straightened, her face becoming serious. "I can understand that, but now you're divorced, it might do you good to start dating again."

Ben stared out the window. *Dating?* Was he ready for that? He fingered the faint indentation where his wedding band had once sat. He still thought of Kathryn. Her leaving had come as a shock—she'd never told him she was unhappy. How had he missed the signs? He'd been working long hours and maybe hadn't paid her enough attention, but he still couldn't understand how she could have walked out on Jayden like she did. *What kind of mother could do that to her child?* What had they done so wrong to make her leave? A dull ache settled in his chest. No, he wasn't ready to date again. What was he thinking?

Stephanie studied him, awaiting his response.

He stood slowly and walked to the window, placing his hands on the ledge. Below, the street bustled with people either going to or coming back from their lunch break. That's where he needed to be. Work. Where he was busy and could keep his mind active and off Kathryn. *And Tessa.*

No, he needed to let go of her, not that there was anything to let go of. He wasn't ready to even think about dating. Maybe he never would be. He turned and picked up his briefcase. "No, I don't think I can. I need to get back to work, Ms. Trejo. Thanks for your time."

～

STEPHANIE RESTED her elbows on her desk and held her head in her hands. She'd gotten so close, but not close enough. She let out a frustrated sigh. Would Ben ever trust her enough to open up to her? She glanced at her watch. Gwen was due in twenty minutes. Just enough time to snatch a quick bite to eat and a coffee and review her notes from their previous session.

Gwen was another one causing her grief. It didn't seem to make any difference what she said, Gwen was still determined to have her double mastectomy. Seemed she was more concerned about an illness she might never get than saving her marriage. Her husband had stopped coming with her, and according to Gwen, was already making plans to move out.

How could someone who said they trusted God be so self-absorbed and uncaring about their marriage? But then again, her husband didn't seem willing to understand Gwen's fears, either. They'd hit a brick wall and neither was willing to budge. Stephanie shook her head. Some marriages seemed such hard work. If only Gwen and her husband were prepared to really listen to each other, but both were as stubborn as the other. Stephanie had just about given up with them, but she knew that wasn't good enough. She prayed that today there might be a breakthrough of some kind.

She'd just finished her sandwich and coffee when Gwen called. She was sorry for the late notice, but she wasn't going to make it today. In fact, she wouldn't be coming back. Her operation was booked for the following week, and her husband had already moved out.

"Oh, Gwen, I'm so sorry to hear that. Is there... is there anything I can do to help?" Stephanie was almost lost for words. Gwen's news, although not unexpected, was a shock all the same.

"No, I don't think so. I got a cancellation, and now it's happening, Tom just walked out. I'm almost glad, as he's hardly said a word to me for weeks. I'll just be relieved to have it done." Gwen's voice caught in her throat.

"You must be nervous, and a little sad. Please remember I'm here if you want to talk about it either before or after the operation. And I'll keep praying for you and Tom. I don't believe this is the end for you. Maybe he just needs time to get used to it."

"Thank you, Stephanie, I'll keep it in mind."

Stephanie grimaced. *No you won't... you're just saying that.*

After the phone call ended, Stephanie tried to finish Gwen's case study report, but her feeling of failure didn't help one little bit and she struggled to write more than a couple of paragraphs. She sighed and slipped the file into her briefcase. *Another one to take home.*

CHAPTER 6

As she did most Sunday mornings, Tessa sat in the passenger seat beside Stephanie on the way to church. She didn't feel like talking, so she just sat there and gazed out the window.

Despite returning to work and having Sparky welcome her home every night with more kisses than she could cope with, she still couldn't shake the dullness that weighed her down most days and nights. Although she sought God's guidance and direction every day, her heart was heavy and she struggled to remain positive. The joy of the Lord had most definitely eluded her. She was drifting, and she didn't like it.

The truth was, her weekends had become boring without Michael. They'd always done exciting and fun things on their days off, but now, everything was mundane. Sparky provided the only brightness in her life. Her heart warmed a little as she pictured him running around with the other dogs the previous afternoon at the off-leash area. He'd had such fun! But while she'd been there, her focus had been drawn to the happy couples riding along the cycle path beside the river, and memories of the times she and Michael had ridden along those same paths made her melancholy again. Maybe she should go for a ride, but riding on her own didn't appeal. Stephanie wouldn't come, so no use asking her. Maybe Elliott. But even if he agreed, it wouldn't be the same.

"Hey, what's up?" Stephanie cast her a concerned look as she brought the car to a stop at a red light. "You're very quiet. Is everything okay?"

Tessa shrugged and spoke quietly as she shifted her gaze to the front and picked at her nails. "Yes, I'm fine. Just a little down, that's all."

"Some good old-fashioned worship should do us both good."

"You're probably right." She turned her head and smiled fondly at her friend. Despite Steph's outward cheeriness, Tessa knew that work was causing her a great deal of stress and most nights she'd come home and spend hours poring over her cases. She was even wondering if she'd chosen the right career path and whether she'd finish her course.

They arrived early as it was Stephanie's week to play the organ. Tessa chatted with several of the older church members as well as her parents while she waited for the service to begin. Although she loved the older members dearly, many of whom she'd known since she was a little girl, occasionally she went to one of the larger churches where the congregation on average was younger. But whenever she'd seriously considered a permanent change, pangs of guilt hit her. Gracepointe was home.

Here she'd learned about Jesus and the Bible, and the Sunday-school classes she'd attended had paved the way for her eventual decision to give her heart and life to Christ. Yes, Gracepointe was home, and now as she stood to sing *How Great Is Our God* with the rest of the congregation, her soul lifted, and she reaffirmed her commitment to follow Christ. She also apologised again to God for being so down and not trusting Him enough.

After the service was over, she had a cup of tea and chatted again with her parents and several other members of the church about this and that. She then settled back down in the sanctuary to wait for Stephanie who was accompanying the choir as they practiced for an upcoming concert.

As she sat in an empty pew listening to the sweet sounds coming from the choir, Tessa's mind drifted to Ben. Despite her promise to God not to think of him, she couldn't help it. She'd struggled to keep her thoughts off him and looked forward to seeing him and Jayden again at their next puppy training class.

She jumped when Gracepointe's long-time pastor appeared beside her. She hadn't heard him come in, so lost she'd been in her thoughts. "Waiting for Stephanie?" he asked.

Tessa nodded and gave him a smile.

"You look deep in thought. Is everything okay?" His kindly voice warmed her heart, but she felt a pang of guilt as her mind had been on Ben and Jayden, and not on God. Just as well he couldn't read her mind. "Yes, it is. Thank you. I enjoyed your message today. I really needed to be reminded that God's in control even when I don't understand His plans."

"Well, I'm pleased to hear that. I always pray that my preaching will draw my congregation closer to God and encourage them in their walk." The ingrained lines around the pastor's eyes creased further as he patted her hand and returned her smile.

When tears pricked her eyes, she tried to push them away. Why did she always get emotional around him? Maybe it was his kindly manner, but he managed to get below her surface so easily, and it was embarrassing. She chastised herself and lowered her head so he couldn't see her moist eyes.

"Is there anything in particular I can help you with or pray about before I leave?"

She shook her head but then stopped. She was so used to doing that—saying she was fine when she wasn't, saying *no* when she meant *yes*, and *yes* when she meant *no*. Maybe she should talk with him. After all, he knew her as well as anyone. In fact, he probably knew her better than most, possibly even more than her parents did.

She wiped her eyes with her other hand and took a deep breath. "There is something you might be able to help me with." She lifted her eyes and looked into his kindly face. "I know this might sound silly, but after my breakup with Michael, I've been wondering how I'll know when God brings the *right* person into my life. I'd always thought Michael was the one, but then…" Her voice faltered, and she swallowed the lump that had climbed into her throat.

"Ah, Tessa. It's dangerous for people to think that God has one perfect person out there for them to marry. Of course, God already knows who you'll marry, if indeed you marry at all. But if you search endlessly for the *right* one, you'll probably never find him because there is no perfect spouse." Pausing, he indicated they should sit.

"Too often people expect God to miraculously bring the right person into their lives, but that's usually not what He does. God leaves it entirely up to us to make a wise choice. He's set only one condition—and that is that believers should marry fellow believers.

"I'll give you the same advice I gave to your mother when she wanted to know if your father was the right one for her."

Tessa looked up, wondering if she'd heard right. *Mum had doubts about marrying a man as loving, strong, and hard-working as Dad? No. He must have gotten her confused with someone else.*

"Ask God to give you wisdom and discernment in your relationships," he continued. "Regardless of what interests you may share, keep Christ at the centre of all you do, and ground yourself in His Word. Make sure that the one you run after is running after God. And pray, Tessa. Pray for God to prepare you for your husband. Pray for God to prepare you to handle all the joys, tears, heartache and commitment that go into making a godly marriage."

She nodded, accepting the fact that although Michael had gone to church, he'd never been committed, and she couldn't say with all honesty that he was running after God. *But was she?* She thought so, but she was running after so many things. Was God her focus? Was she seeking Him with all her heart? If she were honest, she'd have to say no, she hadn't been running after God, even though at times she thought she had. But from now on, she'd make sure she was.

"Tessa, also know that if you remain unmarried, God's love for you doesn't depend on your marital status." She didn't want to hear that. Even though she was racing towards her thirties, remaining single hadn't entered her thinking. She'd always assumed she'd get married and have children. *But what if that doesn't happen?* Could she cope with the loneliness of remaining single—possibly forever? A few months on her own and she was struggling. Her chest tightened at the thought. God would really have to help with that.

"Don't worry, Tessa." He patted her hand. "You've got plenty of time, and I'm sure there's many a young man who'd jump at the chance of spending time with you. Just be discerning and don't rush into anything. Okay?"

She nodded and smiled through the tears blurring her eyes.

"If you don't mind, can I pray for you before we part?"

She sniffed. "That would be lovely. Thank you." She released a slow breath and closed her eyes.

He placed his hand lightly on her shoulder. Streams of sunlight, stained a rainbow of colours by the glass windows of the church, cast a heavenly illumination about them as his gentle voice implored God to shower her with His love and peace, and to give her wisdom and discernment in her relationships.

"Thank you," she said gratefully when he finished.

"Always my pleasure, dear." He squeezed her hand and then stood. "Let me know if you'd like to chat again."

"I will. Thank you."

She had only a few minutes longer to wait before Stephanie came out from choir rehearsal. As they drove home, Tessa felt more at peace than she had since breaking up with Michael, and she pushed any romantic notion about Ben out of her mind.

CHAPTER 7

*S*tephanie sat behind her desk and glanced at the clock on the wall. Ten more minutes until Ben was due. Drumming her fingers on the desk, she leaned back in her chair and sighed deeply. Even though they'd had two meetings a week for the past month, they'd made little progress. She'd been hopeful during last Friday's meeting that things were starting to turn around, but in the end she'd been disappointed when he left abruptly.

"Come in," she said in answer to the knock on her office door.

Rod Casey, her supervisor, entered and sat on a chair on the opposite side of the desk.

Her stomach tightened while she waited for him to speak.

"I received your case studies on Annabel and her brother, as well as Gwen's."

Stephanie held her breath. So much time had been invested in getting those reports right.

"Annabel's was excellent—I was very impressed." He looked up and held her gaze. "But Gwen's?" She didn't like the look on his face. Her heart fell. She'd really struggled to put hers together, especially after the woman cancelled.

"I'm not so happy with that one. You could have shown more empathy and understanding with her situation. I know she cancelled, but I'm going to move her to another case worker for follow up. You can continue working with Annabel."

She couldn't believe it. She felt like a school-girl who'd just been reprimanded and had her privileges withdrawn. She didn't deserve this. Not after all the time she'd put in. And this was supposed to be a Christian counselling service. Where was the support for their workers? No wonder they struggled to keep their staff.

Swallowing her disappointment, she put on her professional voice. "I'm sorry it wasn't what you wanted. I'll do better with the next one." She drew a deep breath and lifted her chin. "Ben Williams' report is due in two weeks? Correct?"

"Yes. I'll email you some pointers, but I'm sure you'll do better with him. I look forward to receiving it."

Despite her show of bravado, as soon as Rod left, Stephanie's shoulders drooped. If he knew how little progress she'd made with Ben, he wouldn't be so confident. The only progress worth noting was that Ben now had a dog. And that she'd finally managed to get more than two words out of him.

A moment later, another knock sounded on her door. Her shoulders drooped further. *He would be early, today of all days.* Maybe she could say she was unwell and postpone the meeting. But that would be running away. No, she could do this.

Standing, she drew a deep breath and smoothed her skirt, adopting her professional manner before responding.

"Come in."

When Ben entered, she welcomed him with a smile she hoped looked warmer than it felt and waved him to his usual chair before taking the opposite seat. She cleared her throat. "How was your weekend?"

He shrugged off-handedly. "It was okay."

How many more times could they go through the same old routine? If only he'd open up. She must be doing something wrong to have made such little progress. Two weeks left to get somewhere... her resolve hardened. She'd make progress today if it killed her. Forcing herself to relax, she softened her voice. "How is Jayden doing?"

He shrugged again and looked down at his hands. "He's fine, I guess. But all he seems to care about now is Bindy." He looked up and met her gaze. "Yesterday, he didn't want to come to church with me. First time that's happened."

"I'm sorry to hear that. How's he doing at school?"

"His grades have improved a little. I'm sure it's because of Bindy. I told him if he didn't pick up his game, he wouldn't be going to puppy classes. Seems to have worked." He ran his hands down his smart trouser pants and then glanced out the window. "But I'm concerned about the friends he's hanging out with at school. They aren't the best of kids."

A crack. Might only be a small one, but it was a crack. And he'd said way more than two words... She smiled to herself. There was hope.

"Jayden's causing you a great deal of stress and worry, isn't he?"

Ben let out a long sigh. "Yes."

A one-word answer. *Drat!* She'd have to make sure she didn't ask questions he could answer with a simple *yes* or *no*. She really was no good at this.

"Let's talk about your work. Are you happy at your current workplace?"

"Yes."

She berated herself. She'd done it again. *Use a different tack, Stephanie.* "Being a sole parent and holding down a full-time job can't be easy. How are you managing?"

He looked at her guardedly. "Okay, I think. I try to get home as early as I can, but sometimes I get held up." He looked out the window and stared into the distance.

Come on, Ben, give me more. You talked to Tessa, why can't you talk to me?

He finally turned his head but gazed down at his hands. "I got offered a partnership last week."

Her brow shot up. "Congratulations! Are you going to accept?"

He raised his head. "I'm not sure. I'd like the challenge, but I don't know if I should. I need to give an answer by the end of the week, after the Accounting Awards."

"Is that like the Grammy's for accountants?"

"Kind of. It's this Friday evening. I was going to take Jayden, but I doubt he'll want to come. It's not really an event for kids."

Stephanie's mind worked overtime. *Maybe he could ask Tess... she'd be so excited. And maybe she could do some sleuthing for me at the same time.*

She cleared her throat. Her heart rate increased. "Perhaps you could ask that woman you met at puppy training to go with you?" She hoped it sounded natural. It sounded contrived to her.

He shook his head. "I don't think so. I've only met her the once. And she'd read too much into it if I did. I'll just go on my own."

Stephanie's shoulders sagged. "Why not ask her? It might do you good."

"No, I couldn't do that. But thanks for the suggestion."

She studied him as he rose. Such a sad sack. A pity, because he's a nice-looking man.

~

FOR THE NEXT TWO DAYS, Stephanie's suggestion played over in Ben's mind. Something about Tessa Scott had touched him even though they'd only met the once. *But could he ask her to the Awards Ceremony? What if she turned him down?*

When he saw her at puppy training school the next evening, he struggled to put two words together. She smiled at him and said hello, but the connection he thought they'd shared the previous week didn't seem to be there. *Probably just as well.* But he'd almost decided to ask her to the awards dinner, and now disappointment sagged through him.

He caught her eye several times during the session, and each time his heart lifted. He might be imagining it, but maybe the connection *was* still there.

After the lesson, he hurried to catch her as she walked briskly to her car. She seemed in a hurry to leave. Maybe he should just let her go. His heart thudded. But it was now or never. He swallowed hard and called out.

She stopped and turned, her eyes lighting up for an instant, but then a look he couldn't decipher flashed across her face.

His hands grew clammy. He held her gaze and willed words to come out of his mouth. "Tessa, how... how are you?"

Her head tilted. "I'm fine. How are you?"

"I'm fine too." He gulped.

Jayden had caught up and stood beside him with Bindy on her leash.

Ben ran his hand through his hair. "Can you take the dogs for a run for a few moments? That's if Tessa doesn't mind."

"Sure." Jayden shot him a puzzled look but took the leash from Tessa and walked off with the two dogs.

"I'm sorry, Tessa. I didn't mean to be presumptuous." Ben shoved his hands into his pockets to hide his nervousness.

Her face broke into that alluring smile and gave him hope. In the dim light of the car park, her eyes sparkled with amusement. She laughed lightly, and he relaxed. "No, it's fine. So, how have you been, really?"

He let out a huge breath. He couldn't remember being this nervous asking Kathryn out. "Not bad. Still working through things. Getting there."

"That's good to hear." She glanced at Jayden trying to untangle the two pups from each other. "Jayden still seems taken with Bindy."

"Yes, he is."

Her eyes lifted to his, and his heart skipped another beat. They chatted about the puppy training sessions and how both pups had improved, but all the while he was waiting for the right opportunity to invite her to the awards dinner. When she asked what he did, he breathed a sigh of relief.

"I'm an accountant." The bemused look on her face surprised him. *Was being an accountant a bad thing?* "I know that sounds boring compared to being a vet, but it's actually really interesting."

She shook her head. "No, no. It's just that my father's an accountant. He says it's a good, stable occupation." She said those last words in a low deep voice, but her eyes shone.

He relaxed a little more. This was it... *but could he do it?* He cleared his throat. "This might sound strange, but the Annual Accounting Awards are coming up, and I wondered if you'd like to accompany me." He'd got it out, but only just. His heart pounded. He'd put himself out there, made himself vulnerable. What would she say?

Her eyes widened and she seemed lost for words.

"I'm sorry. I shouldn't have asked." A heavy weight descended on his chest.

"No, it was just a surprise. When is it?"

He lifted his gaze and hope filled his heart. "This Friday evening. Tomorrow, actually. I'm sorry it's such short notice. I'll understand if you can't..."

"Ben, stop it. I'd love to go."

A wave of relief washed through his body. "You don't know how nervous I was. I expected you to say no."

"Well, I didn't, and I'll look forward to it." Her mouth curved into a smile that reached all the way to her blue eyes and into his heart.

After getting her address and giving her the details, he drove home with Jayden, totally amazed that she'd agreed to go with him.

∽

TESSA ENTERED the house and nearly bumped into Stephanie, who was carrying a load of freshly washed and dried laundry.

"Whoa, what's the rush, and what are you grinning ear to ear about?" Stephanie asked.

"You won't believe it!" Tessa sashayed past her friend and released Sparky onto the floor before continuing.

"Let me guess." Stephanie tilted her head and held a finger to her lips. "Ben asked you out on a date?"

Tessa stopped mid sashay. "How did you know?"

"Maybe because I was the one who suggested it."

"You did—*what?*" She glared at Stephanie, nostrils flaring. All the way home she'd talked to God about Ben, thinking it funny that after deciding he wasn't right for her, it turned out he might be after all. Especially after Stephanie had let slip he was a churchgoer. But knowing she was behind the invitation put a different slant on it altogether.

"Come on, Tess. It doesn't matter how it came about. You're going on a date! Be happy."

Tessa slumped on the couch and crossed her arms. It hurt to discover Ben hadn't asked her out without being prompted. But did it really matter? *Maybe not.* But how would she explain to him that her housemate was his counsellor without him feeling he'd been set up? She humphed. *God, this is way too complicated and I'm not sure what to think. Please help me.*

Stephanie sat on the couch and hugged her. "It'll be all right, you'll see."

CHAPTER 8

"*A*re you sure this looks okay?" The following night, Tessa stood in front of the full-length mirror in her room and fiddled with the navy-coloured sequin mesh gown she hadn't worn since her graduation. At short notice, it was the only thing she could find, and whilst it still fitted her, she was more at home in veterinary scrubs or gym pants.

"Yes, for the hundredth time, you look like a million dollars!" Stephanie shook her head and laughed.

Tessa had finally decided to let go of her annoyance about how or why Ben had asked her out, and just be happy he had. Her heart skipped several beats when the doorbell rang.

"Go on, you'll be fine." Stephanie hugged her. "I'll stay out of sight. Have a great time. But don't forget to find out what you can."

Tessa glared at her. Gleaning information from Ben didn't sit well with her and she'd told Stephanie that. Taking one last look in the mirror, she walked to the front door, her pulse quickening. *God, please be with me tonight. Help me not to read too much into anything, and to keep my eyes on You. Thank You.*

She reached out and opened the door.

Dressed in a sharp black tailored dinner suit that made him look like the accountant he was, Ben stood on the doorstep. She noted the beads of perspiration dotting his forehead, possibly from wearing a suit on a hot summer's evening, but maybe from nerves, just like her.

She swallowed the lump in her throat and smiled. "Ben, hello!"

"Hello, Tess." Their eyes locked together for a moment, as if neither knew what to do or say.

He eventually broke the silence. "You look lovely. And I'm not just saying that. You really do."

She smiled gratefully. "Thank you. You don't look bad yourself." She let out a nervous laugh as he led her to his car. She slid under his arm and onto the passenger seat, sinking deep into the soft leather.

He started the engine and pulled away from the kerb. "Thanks for coming with me." His deep voice sent a tingle through her body. He looked straight ahead and had a firm grip on the steering wheel. "I hope you won't be bored."

"It's nice just going out. I'm sure it'll be fine."

He gave her a warm smile, and they chatted about pups and puppy training for the ten or so minutes it took to get to the Hotel Grand Chancellor in the city.

AROUND FIVE HUNDRED people attended the gala awards night. Under the setting sun, the Roma Street Parklands looked spectacular from the floor to ceiling windows. Ben and Tessa had arrived right on time and he introduced her to his associate, Walton, and several other of workmates and partners who seemed pleased to meet her.

She didn't fully understand all the accounting jargon and financial jokes that were thrown around the table as the evening wore on, but she followed along as best she could and cheered politely whenever the MC mentioned the name of Ben's firm. When it was announced that they'd won the "Firm of the Year" award, the whole table burst into applause. After the CEO made his acceptance speech, the MC went on to announce the "Accountant of the Year" award. He mentioned that the recipient stood out for his innovative client and management ideas. Ben leaned into Tessa and mentioned the name of the person he assumed would be the winner, but when the MC announced it was him, she turned to him with wide eyes and gave him a brief impromptu hug.

His face was a blend of disbelief and delight as Walton clapped him on the shoulder.

She felt nervous for him as he walked to the podium and wondered if he'd prepared a speech. If it had been her, she probably wouldn't know what to say and would speak too fast and say things she ought not. Ben walked confidently to the front of the room, and when he turned to face the applauding audience, her heart swelled with pride, even though she barely knew him.

"Thank you." He waited for the applause to die down. "I'm greatly humbled and honoured to be receiving this award. I'd like to give my deepest gratitude to God. He's blessed me in more ways than I deserve." A hush descended on the room. His voice commanded attention, but mentioning God in a gathering such as this? "I'm also grateful to my partners and my firm." He turned his gaze to his colleagues sitting either side of Tessa. "It's a joy to work with you and for you.

"I'd be lying if I said I'd made the journey here alone. Numerous people have supported me along the way. First, while my parents struggled with managing money for much of their lives, they made sure I had a good education and always supported me in all my endeavours. Even though they're no longer here, I'm eternally grateful for their unwavering guidance and encouragement.

"Secondly, I'm thankful for my family." Ben paused and looked down at the podium. He hesitated before moving on. "We aren't together anymore, but I'd like to acknowledge my former wife, Kathryn. Her support in the early years won't be forgotten. Jayden, my son, who's not here tonight, I'm blessed to be his father.

"I feel very honoured to have won this award. I hope I can live up to it. Thank you all."

Ben's award was the last one given out. When he returned to their table, he asked Tessa if she'd like to dance.

Her heart thudded. "I'd... I'd love to. I'm not sure how good I'll be, but I'll give it a go."

As he placed his hand on the small of her back and led her confidently to the dance floor, she marvelled at how nice it felt.

"My dad once told me," he whispered into her ear, "that the most important rule in dancing is not to step on your partner's toes."

She looked down at her peep toe pumps and laughed. "I think he was right," she said as he led her in a slow waltz to the soft music. His arm was firm around her waist, their faces inches apart. At the base of her throat a pulse beat and swelled as though her heart had risen from its usual place. She wouldn't spoil the night by trying to extract information from him like Stephanie had asked. Let her find it herself.

"I thought your acceptance speech was sincere." Tessa spoke quietly, not quite trusting her voice. "I was pleased to hear that you're a Christian."

He lowered his gaze and met hers. "Yes, since I was eighteen. What about you?"

"Yes, since I was ten. I know that's young, but I'd been brought up in the church and in a Christian family. I don't think I fully understood what I was doing, but I knew it was something I wanted to do, and I haven't regretted it."

"I thought you might have been, but I wasn't sure. I'm glad." His hand firmed on her back as he guided her around a tight corner and between other dancers. She had always dreamed of being swept around a dance floor with a handsome man. How often had she wished Michael could dance like this? But he only ever wanted to jig. He really was such a big kid. Ben was a man, and a smart, handsome one at that.

They continued dancing in companionable silence, comfortable in each other's arms. She was more than happy to allow him to lead, savouring the moment until the music changed.

"Would you like a drink?" He steered her out of the way of a bunch of young people who'd just invaded the floor.

"That would be nice. Yes, thank you."

As she sat at a bar table sipping a sparkling mineral water, she felt it was time to find out about the man who could quickly capture her heart if she let him. Recalling Pastor Stanek's advice, she needed to find out who Ben Williams really was and who or what he was chasing. Now was as good a time as any.

Taking another small sip of her drink, she sent up a quick prayer. It'd be so easy to say the wrong thing and spoil everything. She took a deep breath to steady herself. "Ben..."

He turned his head away from the gardens in the distance and looked at her with those milk chocolate eyes that could just about melt her heart. Was she really game enough to pry into his past? What if she offended him by asking? From what Stephanie had told her, he didn't open up to anyone, and yet, he'd mentioned Kathryn in his speech. Maybe it was just Stephanie he had trouble with.

Her heart quickened, and she clenched her hands together to stop them from shaking. "What happened with your wife? You mentioned her in your speech."

His eyes clouded, his expression altering, like a veil had fallen over his face.

"You don't have to say if you don't want to." She gulped. Had she ruined everything?

He didn't answer, but looked down at his hands. What had happened to the man who'd spoken so confidently in front of that huge crowd? Where had his self-assurance gone?

"It's not something I normally like to talk about," he finally replied. He looked up and held her gaze. "But I don't mind telling you."

She breathed easier. *Thank you, God.*

"There isn't much to tell, really." He glanced out the window and stared into the distance. "Kathryn and I first met in middle school, and then bumped into each other again at church some years later. She'd started going with a bunch of her girlfriends. We married as soon as I finished University. We were both very young, just turned twenty-two." He turned to face her. "I'm not sure how wise we were in doing that, but we loved each other. At least, I thought we did." He lowered his eyes and fiddled with his hands. "I loved her. Kathryn fell pregnant with Jayden in our first year of marriage. I would have loved more children, but she had a difficult pregnancy and didn't want to go through it all again, so we just left it at one." He shrugged as if it didn't matter, but Tessa was sure it did.

"How many children did you want?"

Ben looked up, his eyes a little brighter. "I'd always thought I'd like three. Maybe four." A small smile appeared on his face.

"So after Jayden, what happened?"

The smile slipped and he sighed deeply. "We were married for almost thirteen years, and then one day she told me she'd met someone else and was going to the States to live. A year to the day after she left, she filed for divorce. I haven't seen or heard from her since."

Tessa's heart ached for him. How could anyone do something like that to a man like Ben? "But how could she do that? Just up and leave you both? Especially her son?"

Ben's gaze shifted back to the gardens. He looked so sad, as if he was carrying the weight of the world on his shoulders. The hurt from Kathryn's leaving was written all over his face, making her breakup with Michael look like nothing.

"I'm still trying to find the answer to that question."

Reaching out her hand, Tessa placed it lightly on his. "I'm so sorry, Ben. I truly am."

CHAPTER 9

"Would you like to take a walk?" Tessa asked Ben softly as she looked into his melancholy eyes. She was still struggling to process what he'd told her about Kathryn. It was no wonder he was struggling; it was beyond belief.

"I think I'd like that. Some fresh air would be good." He gave her a wan smile.

They said goodbye to his associates and left the hotel.

The balmy evening air embraced them as they crossed the street from the hotel to the Roma Street Parklands. Ben carried his jacket over his arm and loosened his tie. Beside him, Tessa inhaled the lingering scent from the tropical plants lining the walkways. The clear sky overhead was littered with twinkling stars.

"I meant to ask about him earlier, but how's Jayden doing? I know he's doing well with Bindy, but what about everything else?"

Ben groaned and shook his head. "Getting harder to handle. I guess it's to be expected at his age."

"He must have been upset when his mum left."

"He was shattered. When I first told him Kathryn had gone, he thought I was joking and that she'd just gone to the store and would be back any minute. But as the days turned into weeks and she didn't come back, he knew I was telling the truth." Ben stopped and leaned on the railing of a small bridge. "She called him once or twice. He cried each time, but then he clammed up. He couldn't understand why she'd left." The deep hurt in Ben's eyes brought tears to Tessa's. "He had a few angry outbursts, but he basically withdrew into himself. He hasn't been the same boy since she left."

"Does he ever talk about it?"

Ben sighed heavily and shook his head. "He used to ask if his mum left because of him. I assured him it had nothing to do with him, but I don't think he believed me. He's carrying a lot of bitterness and anger, but he refuses to talk about it with me or anyone else."

"I'm not surprised he's still struggling. That's a horrible thing to have happen. Have you thought about arranging some counselling for him?"

"Yes, but he's not ready. It would be pointless at the moment."

Tessa was tempted to say 'much like yours', but thought better of it. "I'll pray for him. It's the least I can do."

"Thank you. I appreciate that."

They continued strolling along the pathway in silence. After a few moments, she asked if he had any plans to change jobs. "You'll be in demand after winning that award."

Ben chuckled. "Maybe, but I enjoy where I am at the moment. They're good people. In fact, I've just been offered a partnership. I don't think I'll take it—Jayden's my priority right now, not my work, but it was a nice feeling to be given the opportunity. What about you? Do you enjoy your work?"

"I love it. I think I'd like to have my own practice one day."

"Big dreams. I like it. Jayden told me the other night on the way home from puppy school that he wants to be a vet, just like you. So that's something."

"Really?" That surprised her. He'd hardly said two words to her.

"Yes, instead of a rock star, so that's saying a lot."

She laughed. "He's already good with Bindy and Sparky. I'm sure he'd be a great vet if he decided to give up his rock star dreams!"

They came to a bench beside a water feature and took a seat. "Is Jayden a believer?"

"He comes to church with me, but I get the feeling he'd rather not. I wish he'd see his need for God, and I'm praying he will, sooner rather than later."

"People often have a hard time believing when so many bad things happen to them. I'll pray for him too."

"Thank you."

"I know you probably don't feel this way," she said, turning to look him in the eye. "But you're doing a great job with Jayden. I've watched you in training classes, and you're so patient and thoughtful with him. You're a wonderful dad."

His eyes moistened as he searched her face. "You really think so?" His voice was quiet, disbelieving.

"I do." She smiled.

He covered her hand with his own and squeezed it. They sat together in silence and listened to the water swish under the bridge beside them as rainbow lorikeets flitted back and forth between the trees. She couldn't think of any place she'd rather be.

A SHORT TIME LATER, Ben straightened and looked at his watch, alarm spreading across his face.

"What's wrong, Ben?"

"Jayden had rugby practice tonight. I was meant to pick him up around 9.30." He thumped his head. "I totally forgot, and now I'm almost an hour late."

"Has he called?"

"Probably. I turned my phone to silent before the awards ceremony." He took his phone out and grimaced. "Nine missed calls." He hit Jayden's number, but it went straight to voicemail. He left a message, apologising profusely and telling him to stay put and that he'd be there as soon as possible.

They hurried from the parklands, recrossing the street to the Hotel Grand Chancellor's parking lot and found his car. The drive back to Tessa's place was largely a quiet one.

Pulling into her driveway, he left the engine running and turned to her. "I'm sorry we had to end this outing so abruptly, but thank you again for coming. I really enjoyed your company." When his eyes settled on hers, she had a hard job controlling her thoughts. All she wanted was for him to take her in his arms. "Maybe we could do it again sometime soon. Not at a ceremony, of course. Just you and me."

Had she heard right? He was asking her out on a proper

date? She smiled warmly at him. "I'd like that. Thank you." Her pulse quickened as he leaned over and kissed her cheek, his soft lips brushing her skin.

"Goodnight, Tess."

"Goodnight, Ben." Her mouth went dry, and she wasn't sure if he heard her.

~

"Tess, will you put that phone down and finish telling me what happened." Stephanie sat cross-legged on the couch in their living room.

Tessa sat across from her on another couch with Sparky curled in her lap. She'd exchanged her gown and heels for a white shirt dress and bare feet. As soon as she read the brief text message from Ben, she set her phone aside and rehashed some of the night's events, leaving out any information that could be classified as private and confidential.

"Come on, Tess, give me more. You know I need more than I've got to put in my report."

"No, it's not right. And besides, I'm just getting to know him so I don't know much. Sorry."

"Okay then. But tell me, has he asked you out again?"

"Maybe." But Tessa knew that the playful grin on her face gave it away.

~

BEN WAITED until Tessa was safely inside before he accelerated down the street and headed towards Jayden's school, a good twenty minute drive away. No doubt she'd be having second thoughts about his parenting skills after this. But it didn't really matter what anyone else thought. He'd failed both as a husband and as a father. He hadn't been able to keep his wife, and now he was certain he was losing his son—slowly but surely.

The grassy sports field belonging to the middle school was empty and shrouded in darkness when he arrived. Everyone had left for the night. Not surprising really—he was well over an hour late.

Jayden must have caught a ride with one of his friends. Ben dialled his number again as he headed home. It rang several times before once again going to voicemail. He was calling for the fifth time when he entered the kitchen via the garage.

Jayden was at the microwave warming up leftover Hawaiian pizza slices and shot him angry daggers. "Where were you? I called you like a zillion times, and you're now just calling me back?"

"I'm sorry. My phone was on silent and I lost track of time. How did you get home?"

"What do you care?" He flicked his hair off his face. "I got a lift with Neil, if you want to know."

The microwave beeped. He yanked the door open, snatched the pizza slices out and slid them onto a plate.

Ben tried to think of something else to say but couldn't. Jayden was upset with him, and this time, he couldn't blame the boy. "I'm sorry, son. It won't happen again."

"I don't believe you." Jayden's words stabbed at his heart. He was losing him, and fast. "Obviously your work thing was more important than me." Jayden picked up his plate and headed for the stairs.

"That isn't true." He disappeared before Ben could say more.

As Ben sprinted up the stairs after him, his phone buzzed and he stopped. Maybe it was a good thing. Jayden was in no mood to talk. He looked at the text message. It was from Tessa, asking if everything was all right with Jayden. It wasn't, but he didn't feel like telling her all that had just happened, so he just wrote back 'yes'.

CHAPTER 10

hen Ben's associate, Walton, telephoned early
Saturday morning, Ben was having breakfast
and reading his Bible, searching for guidance and direction.
The previous evening's upset with Jayden still hung heavily on
his heart.

"Something's come up, and I won't be able to make the Pro-
Am Golf Tournament with you and Jayden today." He sounded
apologetic.

Ben leaned back in his chair. "That's a pity. I know how
much you were looking forward to it."

"I know, but it's unavoidable. Why don't you invite Tessa to
go along with you so the ticket won't go to waste?"

Ben blinked. *Invite Tessa? She mightn't like golf. And she
mightn't want to see me again so soon, especially after the fiasco with
Jayden. But why not?* His heart thumped at the prospect of
seeing her again so soon. "I might just do that. You don't have
anyone else who could use it?"

"No no. You take it. My pleasure."

"Thanks, mate. Enjoy your day, whatever you're doing."

"I will."

Ben dialled Tessa's number as soon as he got off the phone from Walton. He almost hit stop when it began ringing. His pulse quickened. What was he doing? He wasn't thinking straight. But it was too late. She'd see his number and know he'd rung. After two rings, she answered in a sleepy voice.

He groaned. "Did I wake you? I'm so sorry."

"I was half-awake. It's not a problem," She stifled a yawn.

"I know it's short notice, but I was hoping you might come with me to the Pro-Am today. The friend I was going with has just cancelled, and so I've got a spare ticket and I thought you might like to come."

A long silence followed. His heart sank. Why had he been so rash? Of course she wouldn't want to go. What had he been thinking?

More moments passed. After what seemed a life-time but was probably only a second, she asked, "Is that the golf tournament?"

He breathed a sigh of relief. "Yes, it is. I guess you don't follow golf?"

"No, but I'd love to come anyway. I'd only planned on doing a spot of shopping, but that's not important."

Had he heard right? She'd love to come? His spirits soared and he punched the air. "Great! I'll pick you up at eight."

Next, he needed to wake Jayden. How he'd kept it a secret from him for so long, Ben wasn't sure, but how good to have this up his sleeve right now. Even though Jayden didn't play golf, he'd developed an interest in watching it on television, and Ben was sure he'd love to see a professional match.

He ran up the stairs, paused outside Jayden's door, and knocked softly.

"*Leave me alone.*"

Ben clenched his fists. It was the tone he'd come to detest. He needed every inch of self-control not to react. "You'd better get up if you want to go to the Pro-Am today." He held his breath, waiting for Jayden's response.

Within moments, the bedroom door was yanked open. Jayden, bare-chested and wearing only pyjama bottoms, stood in the doorway, mouth agape. "Today? You've got tickets?"

"I do," Ben answered smugly. "Tee off's in just over an hour, so we'll need to leave soon."

"Okay, I'll get ready and be straight down."

Ben returned downstairs with a skip to his step. Maybe things between him and Jayden were fine again. *At least for a while.* It was foolish to think a day's outing would fix every-thing, but at least it was something. And Tessa was coming... the thought of her sitting beside him all day put a wide grin on his face. *Thank you, God.* Having her beside him might also stop him thinking of Kathryn.

If she'd been here, Kathryn would have been front row. Luke Emerson was playing today. Not only had Luke been Kathryn's favourite golfer, he'd been her favourite athlete, period, almost to the point of obsession. Whenever she couldn't see him play live, she'd watch all his tournaments on television. Magazines that featured him littered the house. Kathryn had been star-struck, and Ben hadn't liked it. The guy was a wealthy play boy. Everyone knew it. Kathryn didn't care.

Luke Emerson was definitely not Ben's favourite golf player. Although the man had a keen style and Ben enjoyed watching him play, whenever Ben heard his name mentioned, thoughts of Kathryn returned as well and painful memories came flooding back. But he couldn't let the free tickets go to waste, and so just for today, he'd put aside his dislike for the man and enjoy his time with Jayden and Tessa.

He poured himself another coffee and drank it slowly while waiting for Jayden to come down. Thinking of Kathryn always left him melancholy. The initial shock of her leaving had been replaced with a heavy dull ache. If only he knew where he'd gone wrong. She hadn't even given him the opportunity to talk about it, to give him a chance to fix whatever the problem was. It was too late to fix it, but if he knew what he'd done, he might be able to deal with it and move on. Not knowing *why* had torn him inside. So many emotions he hadn't sorted out. So many questions waiting to be answered. He swallowed the lump in his throat and sighed heavily. *God, where did I go wrong?* Maybe he did need to open up with Stephanie and allow her to help him.

"Dad, are you ready?" Jayden's voice brought him back to the present. He was at the counter stuffing buttered toast into his mouth. "I've fed Bindy and I'll walk her tonight. Let's go."

JAYDEN BEGAN TALKING EXCITEDLY EVEN before he jumped into the front seat beside Ben. "Maybe I can get Luke Emerson's autograph today. What do you think?"

Ben pushed back his initial response and tried to answer positively. "Yes, why not? It's worth a try." He flashed Jayden an encouraging smile. He could almost endure anything to have Jayden excited about something.

Jayden's brows puckered. "Where are we going? The golf course isn't this way."

Ben had been waiting for that. His smile faded. "You remember Tessa, the lady from puppy school?" He held his breath as he waited for Jayden's response.

Jayden turned his head, his eyes puzzled.

A sinking feeling flowed through Ben's body and settled in his stomach. Why hadn't he mentioned up-front that Tessa was coming? He gulped. "I invited her to come with us." He tried to sound upbeat about it.

Jayden remained silent. There was no need for words, the daggers in his eyes said it all.

"I'm sorry. I should have told you."

Jayden crossed his arms and slunk down in his seat. "No, you shouldn't have asked her."

Ben's shoulders fell. "I thought you liked her?"

"Not that much."

WHEN TESSA CLIMBED into the back seat a short while later, she leaned forward and smiled brightly as she wished Jayden good morning. Ben had warned her he wasn't in a good mood, but hadn't explained why.

"Morning." Jayden's voice was short and crisp. He turned his head and stared out the window. He said nothing more for the entire trip.

She hoped it was because he was still unhappy about being

forgotten, but she had an inkling it might be because she was intruding on his time with his father. Maybe she shouldn't have come…

When they arrived, the golfing complex was already filled with a throng of people. Not just spectators and fans, but sports' reporters, news media and photographers. The Pro-Am Golf Tournament was a big event, so it seemed.

Tessa tagged along behind Ben and Jayden to watch Luke Emerson, whoever he was, tee off on the first hole. Jayden didn't seem interested in seeing anyone else play; he just wanted to see Luke. The threesome followed him and his amateur partner from hole to hole throughout the morning.

"Luke's the best player around these days," Jayden informed her enthusiastically on their move to the fourth hole.

She was so glad he was finally talking to her, and she asked questions to keep him engaged. "I've never been to either, so what's the difference between a Pro-Am tournament and a regular tournament?"

"Pro tour golfers and ordinary golfers play together at Pro-Ams. It's still a competition, and the winning team still gets the prize, but they usually raise money for charity at the same time."

"Oh, look," Ben said, holding up the event brochure he'd been reading. "This year the Pro-Am is supporting several Australian animal charities."

"Cool." Jayden's face lit up. "Bet you're happy about that, Tessa."

"Absolutely." She smiled affectionately at him, thankful he'd forgiven her for gatecrashing his day with his dad.

CHAPTER 11

*W*hen the players paused for lunch, Luke Emerson was at the top of the leaderboard. "I'll try to get his autograph now, and maybe a photo. Wanna come?" Jayden asked Ben as the crowd around Luke began to disperse.

"No, you go, son." Ben gave him an affectionate squeeze.

"Save my lunch," Jayden called as he ran off.

As Tessa strolled with Ben to the grill, the need to come clean with him sat heavily on her mind. Now was as good a time as ever. But would he understand it hadn't been a conspiracy? Maybe Stephanie had intended to use her to glean the information she needed, but Tessa's intentions were honest. Would he believe that? She took a deep breath, but her heart thumped heavily in her chest. *What if he takes it the wrong way? I wouldn't blame him if he did.*

"Ben, I have something to tell you."

He turned his head, meeting her gaze with a puzzled expression. "What is it?"

She gulped. "One thing I try to have in all my relationships is honesty, and so I want to be honest with you."

He lifted an eyebrow. "Are you going to tell me you've got two heads or something?"

She laughed. "No, nothing like that." She paused as she tried to gather the right words. Was there any way to break the news to him about Stephanie without jeopardising their friendship? She somehow doubted it. She looked deep into his eyes. "I'm not quite sure how to say this, so I'll just say it. Your counsellor, Stephanie, is my best friend."

His head jerked up, his eyes widening as the colour drained from his face.

"I'm so sorry. I didn't know how to tell you." She reached out and grabbed his wrist. He pulled it away. Her chest heaved. It was over. He'd never trust her now.

His eyes held hers, as if he was searching her soul, condemning her. *Say something, please...*

Placing his hand firmly on her elbow, he steered her to the side of the walkway, away from the crowd, and faced her. Hurt and disappointment filled his eyes, and she just wished she could fix it and make it right. "That's not what I expected to hear, Tessa. I'm disappointed. So much for client confidentiality." His voice was crisp, and she felt like a naughty school girl.

"Oh, Ben." She swallowed a sob. "I've known Stephanie since we were kids, and now we're house mates. I try not to listen when she talks about her cases. In fact, I try to stop her, but sometimes she just needs to get them off her chest." She implored him with her eyes to understand. "When I met you at puppy school and realised who you were, I was caught. But I didn't think it would matter. Until you asked me out." She lowered her head and stifled a sniff. "Maybe I shouldn't have accepted."

"I should have known there was a connection by the way she kept suggesting I ask you. I should report her."

Tessa looked up, her breath catching. *No! Please don't do that...* A heavy weight settled on her chest. Moments passed.

His expression eased. "But I won't."

Relief flowed through her. His eyes remained steady, but the darkness had lifted a little and his face had softened. "I haven't been the most cooperative of patients. But you probably know that already."

She gave a small nod, afraid to say anything.

"I'm glad you agreed to go out with me, Tess. Even if I was set up."

Without thinking, she reached out and touched his wrist again. "Oh Ben. Don't think of it like that. Please. I didn't say *yes* because of Stephanie. I said *yes* because I wanted to." She bit her lip as she waited for his response.

After several long moments, he placed his other hand on top of hers and rubbed his thumb gently against her skin. "To be honest, I've been hesitant to get involved with another woman again, so I'm glad she pushed me. I may never have asked you out if it hadn't been for her."

All the tension in Tessa's body fell away and a smile, flowing from deep within, grew on her face and reached her eyes. They'd survived their first spat and come out the other side. It could have ended so badly. Their eyes were locked. Her breathing quickened. Was he about to kiss her?

She laughed to herself when he said they needed to order lunch. The kiss would have to wait.

TESSA ORDERED a chicken sandwich and bottled water. Ben ordered the same for himself and Jayden, but added a candy bar as well. They were on their way to a group of shaded picnic tables when Jayden raced towards them, face flushed.

When he didn't stop, Ben leapt from the table and raced after him, pulling on his T-shirt to make him stop. Tessa leaned forward to get a clearer view. What could have upset Jayden so much? Surely he wouldn't have gotten so upset over an autograph?

As Ben attempted to wrap his arms around him, Jayden pulled away. He couldn't stand still and his hands jerked as he jumped from leg to leg. He looked distressed, like he could burst into tears at any moment.

Tessa prayed. It was all she could do.

After several minutes, he calmed down and allowed Ben to place his arm around his shoulder. They walked slowly back to the table.

"Tessa, we need to leave." Ben's voice was serious, and his eyes were dark with pain as he gently placed a hand on her shoulder.

She nodded, not knowing what to say. What could possibly have happened?

As they walked towards the car, Ben broke the silence. "Jayden saw his mum."

Tessa's eyes widened. "*Kathryn?*"

"Yes. She's with Luke Emerson. I should have guessed.

Jayden's positive it was her even though she looked different. He reckons she saw him but acted like she hadn't."

"Oh, you poor thing." Tessa stood and tried to hug Jayden, but he pushed her away.

When they reached the car, he slumped into the back seat and used his thumb to scrub Luke's autograph off the golf ball in his hand. "I hate mum. I hate Luke. I don't wanna see either of them ever again."

Ben turned around, the muscles in his neck taut. "Jayden, don't say that." His voice was measured, but Tessa guessed he was almost as upset as Jayden.

"It's true." Jayden slunk further and continued scrubbing.

Her heart ached for them both. She couldn't blame Jayden for the way he felt, but if he held onto that hate, he'd end up hurting more. And she couldn't even start to imagine how Ben must be feeling.

JAYDEN WAS SPRAWLED across his bed, asleep, when Ben went to check on him later that evening. Tear stains dotted his pillow. The room was junky as always, but where posters of Luke Emerson had been hanging that morning, only bare spaces remained. Ben found the posters crumpled in Jayden's trashcan along with torn photos of Kathryn.

His gaze fell back onto Jayden moaning in his sleep, his face troubled as if he were having a bad dream. Ben moved to the bed and sat on the edge. His chest tightened as he stroked Jayden's dark brown hair, now damp with sweat and tears. How could Kathryn have done this to their son? Did she despise them both so much she'd go out of her way to ignore him? *What mother would do that? Did she have no feelings at all?*

The muscles in Ben's neck tensed the more he thought about it. How dare she do this! He inhaled deeply to control his anger. *God, forgive me, but right now I feel like grabbing her by the throat and dragging her here so she can see what she's done.* His chest heaved and tears pricked his eyes. "I love you, Jayden. I'm so sorry for everything, but I'm here for you. I really am." He choked on his words; tears poured down his cheeks as everything inside him ached for Jayden. If only he could do something to fix it.

Much later, Ben wiped his face and placed a gentle kiss on Jayden's cheek before leaving the room quietly.

CHAPTER 12

*K*athryn leaned forward in one of the luxurious armchairs in the lobby of the hotel where she and Luke were staying, crossing one long leg over the other. Her hands shook as she opened the gold inlaid cigarette case Luke had presented her with on the anniversary of their first year together, just one of the many extravagant gifts he'd bestowed on her in the past year. She was about to light up when she remembered the non-smoking rules of the hotel.

Sighing with frustration, she returned the cigarette to the case and snapped the lid shut. Maybe she should just go to their suite where smoking was allowed on the balcony. *But Luke wouldn't be happy if she went up without him.*

She caught his eye as he signed yet another autograph for the adoring fans gathered in the lobby. In the past, she would have been amongst that group, but now, she could get Luke Emerson's autograph any time she wanted. Her gaze lingered on him as he turned his attention to his fans. What an amazing ride they'd had. And how lucky she'd been to capture this legendary man's heart. Her gaze travelled beyond him to the ballroom where it had all happened. What a night it had been! One of fifty lucky fans chosen to have a private dinner with Luke Emerson on his last visit to Brisbane, and out of those fifty people who'd dined with him that night, he had been captivated by her. *Her!* All night her heart had beaten so fast she was surprised it hadn't exploded. Luke sat at her table and talked with *her*. He asked a lot of questions, and somehow she answered them all. He'd treated her like she was the only person in the room. How special she'd felt. Ben had never made her feel like that. And her body had never felt so alive as it had that night with Luke.

But seeing Jayden today had thrown her world into a spin. She shouldn't have come back to Brisbane with Luke, but he'd insisted. No way could she tell him the real reason for not wanting to come. If she did, he'd dump her there and then. No, it was paramount he never found out about Jayden.

She forced a smile on her face when he called her over for a photograph. How could she refuse? She'd tried so hard to hide her identity from the media, but no doubt it would come out eventually, possibly even tomorrow when the paper came out. And then? Pushing down the sick feeling in the pit of her stomach, she smiled for the cameras. Luke's toned arm around her shoulders offered some comfort, but didn't fully alleviate the dread she felt.

"All right, baby. I'm done for now." He placed a quick kiss on her cheek and waved once more to his fans before linking her arm in his and walking to the elevators. Once the doors closed, he pulled her close. His red polo shirt was slightly damp with sweat, but neither the dampness nor his body odour offended her. In fact, her body still tingled with anticipation whenever he touched her.

"How did I do out there, sweet pea?"

"Fantastic as always." She lifted her head and gazed into his eyes. "But you need to rest. You hardly got any sleep last night."

"I wonder why?" A cheeky grin grew on his face. He squeezed her bottom as the doors opened.

"Luke! Behave!" She giggled as she batted her eyelashes and shimmied her bottom away from him, for a moment forgetting all about Jayden.

Reaching their penthouse suite, he showered and then fell into bed, pulling her with him. After they'd made love, he lay back and pulled her tight.

As he slept soundly beside her, she ran perfectly manicured nails slowly across his chest. If only they could stay here, cocooned in this sumptuous suite, away from the prying eyes of the media and fans. *And Jayden.* As much as she tried to push thoughts of him from her mind, the image of her son's distraught face when recognition hit taunted her. Just as well she and Luke were flying out first thing in the morning, otherwise the temptation to see him might be too great.

She wriggled carefully out of Luke's tight embrace and ran the bath. As the hot, soapy, perfumed water swirled over her body, Kathryn rested her head on the rim of the tub. For the first time since leaving Ben and Jayden, tears sprang to her eyes and rolled down her cheeks.

Had she made the right choice? She opened her eyes slowly

and stared at the soft lights glowing above her. Ben had been so shocked when he saw the packed bags sitting just inside their front door that day. He looked like he'd been punched in the stomach. He'd begged her to reconsider, to change her mind—if for no reason other than Jayden.

He'd pleaded with her to tell him why. What had he done wrong? The problem with that question was that he hadn't done anything wrong. Ben was a good man. He wasn't as good looking as Luke Emerson. He didn't have money in the millions or a mansion or a yacht. He hadn't showered her with attention or lavish gifts like Luke had, and he'd never been as romantic as Luke. But despite all that, Ben was a good man. The problem was, he hadn't made her feel special like Luke had. Luke loved her, and with him, all her dreams had come true.

It had been a mistake having a child. She'd been so young and had no idea what parenthood involved, nor how much she'd have to sacrifice. Ben had been a great father, doting on Jayden and doing everything for him. Just as well, because she couldn't stand the smell of dirty nappies or the feel of sticky fingers. Yes, Jayden was better off without her in his life. But something deep down tugged at her. Jayden was her son. Her flesh and blood. Her eyes burned with unwelcome tears as pain stabbed her heart. She glanced at her phone. Maybe she should call him.

She picked up the phone and dialled the number that was etched in her memory before she changed her mind. As the phone began to ring, Luke called out. She hung up quickly and tried to still her thumping heart. "Coming…"

As she climbed back into bed with him, tucking herself

close to his warm body, she convinced herself she'd made the right decision. Jayden was better off without her.

∽

BEN WOKE early Sunday morning with Jayden's words ringing in his head: *'I saw Mum. She's with Luke.'* Unable to return to sleep, Ben rose and went downstairs. He poured a cup of coffee, picked up his Bible and sat at the kitchen table. Kathryn's leaving hadn't stopped him praying and reading God's Word each morning, but most times, like today, he only read with his eyes; his mind and his heart were a million miles away. He still believed God was in control of everything, but the divorce had certainly tested, if not shaken his faith.

Putting his cup down, he sighed deeply as he rested his head on his upturned hand. The intense pain he'd felt when Kathryn first left had lessened to a dull ache inside his chest, but seeing her with Luke had shocked him. At least now he had some idea as to *why* she'd left. She'd always been spoiled. As an only child of well-to-do parents, she only had to ask and anything she wanted would be hers. That was most likely where he'd failed. He'd never missed her birthday or their anniversary, but he'd never pandered to her or showered her with lavish gifts like Luke most likely had. Maybe if he'd paid her more attention she wouldn't have left. She was always going to the doctor for one thing or another, and he'd often accused her of being a hypochondriac. Ben gulped as he recalled some of the things he'd said to her, but never had he expected her to walk out on him. *Or on Jayden.* Pain gripped his chest. How terrible it must have been for Jayden to discover that his mum had run off with Luke Emerson. But worse still, the fact that she was in town and had chosen not to see him... *How could she do that?*

Thumping rock music and Bindy's barking snapped Ben out of his thoughts. How long had he been sitting there? He looked at the clock. Fifteen minutes to get to church. Closing his Bible, he inhaled deeply before hurrying up the stairs to Jayden's room.

"What?" Jayden called out when Ben knocked on his door before opening it. He was sitting up in bed with his MacBook Air propped on a pillow in front of him.

"Can you turn it down a little?"

Jayden rolled his eyes but complied.

"Better get ready for church."

"I'm not going."

Ben's body slumped. *Not again.* "We went through this last week, Jayden. Let's not go through it again."

"I don't see why I should have to go. It's boring and I don't understand half of what's said." Jayden glared at him. "Besides, you and Mum always went to church, and look where that got us."

Ben's heart dropped. He felt like he'd just been punched. "You can't blame God for Mum leaving."

"God?" Jayden looked up with mocking eyes. "Come on, Dad. After Mum left, I heard you pray every night for God to bring her back. In case you haven't noticed, He hasn't done so. Obviously, He sent her to Luke. I don't think a God who refuses to answer a prayer like yours deserves to be trusted."

"Jayden..."

"I'm not going."

Ben sighed heavily. He couldn't blame Jayden for feeling that way. Hadn't he held those very thoughts himself on occasion? The hurt and defiance in Jayden's face was breaking his heart, but he wouldn't let it go.

"Jayden, you're coming, and that's that."

CHAPTER 13

*T*he previous afternoon, after Ben dropped Tessa off unexpectedly early, she made some coffee and curled up on the living room couch. Her thoughts and prayers were with him and Jayden. How she wished she could do more, but really, what could she do? Stephanie would quiz her, of that she was certain, but no way would she say anything about what had happened.

Shortly after, Stephanie arrived home with the week's groceries, her forehead puckering as she dumped the bag onto the kitchen counter. "I didn't expect you back so soon. Wasn't it an all-day thing?"

Tessa gave an off-handed shrug and just told her Ben had decided to leave early.

Stephanie began to unpack the groceries, but stopped and joined her on the couch. "Is everything all right?"

Tessa caught her friend's gaze. She'd have to be very careful with what she said. She half-shrugged again. "I told him that we were friends. He wasn't too happy about it."

Stephanie's jaw dropped and the colour drained from her face. "No..."

"I told you that would happen." *You should sweat, Stephanie... he could easily have reported you.*

"What's he going to do?" Her voice was shallow.

Tessa held her anxious gaze. Moments passed. She recalled the look on Ben's face when she'd broken the news. But then he'd softened, as she would now. "Nothing. You're a very lucky girl."

Stephanie released a huge breath.

"He was disappointed you'd broken client patient confidentiality, but he's prepared to let it go."

"You're not going to tell me anything he said, then?"

"Absolutely not." Tessa picked up a shirt from the washing basket and folded it. If only she could share Ben's heartache with Steph. They could have even prayed for him and Jayden together, but she daren't do anything that might jeopardize her fledgling relationship with him any further. *If they still had a relationship.* Would they be able to pick up where they left off, or had Kathryn's reappearance changed everything?

"Are you going to see him again? You can tell me that, at least."

Tessa drew a deep breath. "I'm not sure." She couldn't look up. She'd always had trouble hiding her emotions, and Steph could read her like a book.

"You're smitten! I can tell. Look at me."

Tessa slowly raised her head and tried to keep her expression neutral, but she knew that concern for Ben and Jayden was written all over her face. No need to look in a mirror.

"Oh Tessa." Stephanie inched closer and wrapped her arms around her. "I didn't mean for you to get so involved. He's got way too much baggage. And your parents would never approve."

"You should have thought about that before you set us up." Tessa struggled to keep her voice steady. Maybe Steph was right and she should forget all about him.

"I'm sorry, kiddo. I really am." Stephanie gave her a hug. "Hey, I just remembered. Your parents called while you were at the Pro-Am and invited you to join them for an early dinner at Bussey's." She glanced at her watch. "They'll be expecting you in an hour."

"Why didn't Mum call my phone?"

"You know how she is... I said I'd let you know, but then I forgot. I'm sorry, I really am."

Tessa's head drooped. As much as she loved them, dinner with her parents was the last thing she wanted to do, especially at Bussey's. They'd want to know what she'd been doing. How could she convince them nothing much had been happening? Maybe Elliott would be there... but that could be worse. Either way, it was too late to pull out now.

She smiled weakly. "Guess I'd better get ready."

SHE CHANGED out of her aqua-coloured jogging suit and into a flower-patterned summer dress and white sandals. Her parents wouldn't have cared too much what she wore, but Tessa always liked to look presentable around them. She'd long admired how her mother managed to dress impressively whatever the occasion.

Her parents, Telford and Eleanor Scott, were seated at a table outside on the deck overlooking the river when she arrived at the café. Her father stood and kissed her cheek. "You made it. I was just about to call you—we thought you'd forgotten."

"Actually, Stephanie's the one who forgot to tell me until about an hour ago." She took the seat between them and smiled warmly at them both. "This is a nice surprise."

"Yes, well, Stephanie is a forgetful one. I'm just glad she remembered to tell you in time," her mother said. "We took Elliott out last week, so now it's your turn."

"I half expected to see him here."

"You look disappointed, honey." Her father squeezed her wrist.

"I just haven't seen much of him since he's been back, that's all." She gave him an assuring smile. "Never mind. I'll catch up with him later."

"We haven't been here for a long time and thought it'd be nice to come back for a visit." Her father's gaze travelled from one side of the busy café to the other.

Yes, she remembered. They'd had many a family meal here at Bussey's Fish Café when she was growing up. *And Michael used to bring me here all the time.* But her parents were unaware of that. Tonight, as usual, the café was full of busy, smiling waitresses and eating, drinking, and chatting diners. The brass ship's bell sitting beside the exit door would no doubt be rung many times. As a young girl, she couldn't wait to ring the bell each time they left, but Michael had taken over that role as an adult. He thought it a hoot.

"I'm surprised they've stayed in business so long. It's not the most convenient location for a restaurant," her mother said.

"Convenient or not, they have the best seafood around." Tessa picked up the menu and engrossed herself in it.

"I hope you're not planning on getting the kids' meal," her mother said with a little laugh. "You're much too old for that now."

"I agree." Tessa placed her menu back down. She knew it back to front. "I think I'll have the clam chowder, shrimp scampi, and a garden salad."

"You've decided for me," her father said. "I'll have the same, along with a side of chips and a tall iced tea."

Her mother ordered a fish taco and seasoned rice. After the waitress took their orders, her parents turned their full attention to her. "How have you been doing, honey?" her mother asked. "Is life treating you well?"

Here goes... "Yes, life's good, thanks Mum. Work's going well. Fran's opening another clinic in New Farm and wants me to manage it."

"That's lovely, dear." Her mother squeezed her hand.

"Does that mean you won't be doing surgery anymore?" Her father's big bushy eyebrows came together. "All that study, and that talent…"

"Don't worry, Dad." Tessa interrupted him. "I'd still be doing some of the surgery. But nothing's been confirmed yet. Fran would really like me to accept her offer, but I haven't decided yet."

"Be sure to pray about it, dear." He patted her hand. "Now,

tell me, how are things with you and that boyfriend of yours? I forget his name?"

How could Dad forget Michael's name? She'd only been going out with him for almost five years. And he'd forgotten they'd broken up. She was sure she'd told him. Maybe early signs of dementia? *Please, God, no...* She sighed inwardly.

"You remember, dear, Tess told us she and Michael broke up a while ago?"

She flashed her mother a grateful smile.

"Humph. Never did like him anyway."

Their food arrived just then and Tessa breathed a sigh of relief, thankful for the reprieve. However, after thanking the waitress, saying grace, and taking a few bites of his shrimp, her father picked up where he'd left off.

"Thought you were crazy about him. I didn't like him, but your mother and I had assumed you'd end up married." He reached for his glass of iced tea and took a sip.

So had I ... But maybe Dad and Elliott had seen something in him she hadn't. What would they think of Ben? She caught herself. They weren't even going out. Why was she thinking like that?

"Things just didn't work out. You know, after his accident and all. It's very sad, but the medication really changed him." The last time they'd been here he'd been off his head. *Why had her parents chosen to come here?*

Her mother leaned across the table and placed a caring hand on hers. "Is there someone else, dear?"

Tessa felt her face begin to flush. Lowering her eyes, she dabbed a napkin to her lips with her spare hand. *How does she know?* "Yes and no."

"Well, tell us, honey. Who is he and what does he do?"

She gulped. How could she answer that? She could tell Dad that Ben was an accountant. He'd be happy about that. He certainly wouldn't be happy if she told him that Ben was divorced and had a thirteen-year old son.

She straightened in her chair and took a deep breath. "Okay. But I'm not going out with him. He's just a friend. Stephanie sort of inadvertently introduced us because he's a client of hers and we both go to the same puppy training classes. And he's an accountant."

Her father raised an eyebrow. "You say this friend of yours is one of Stephanie's clients?"

She grimaced. Why had she blurted that out?

"Stephanie's a counsellor, isn't she? Or learning to be one."

She nodded.

"What's he getting counselling for?"

"Telford! Don't ask questions like that!" Her mother sounded horrified.

Tessa sighed inwardly at her father's immediate scepticism. He could have picked up on the accountant bit, but no… this was going to be harder than expected.

"Ben's a single father," she said quietly. "He's having a few problems with his son and he's still trying to come to terms with his wife walking out on him."

Her father's fork fell to his plate. "Are you telling me you're dating a divorced man?"

"I'm not dating him, Dad. And it isn't like that. He didn't want a divorce. It was all his wife's... *his former wife's*, doing."

"Think twice before getting involved with a divorcee, Tessa. You know what the Bible says about divorce."

Her mother placed a hand lightly on his arm again. Tessa stared down at the small pools of sauce remaining on her empty plate. She'd read through most of the Bible, but struggled to recall the specific verses that talked about divorce. She'd had no need to study them... *until now.* Stephanie was right again. Her parents didn't approve of Ben, and they hadn't even met him.

She looked up. "Not really. But I guess I should."

"Well, Jesus is pretty clear about it in Matthew 19," her father continued. "He said that what God has joined together, no man should separate, and that, except for marital unfaithfulness, anyone who divorces and remarries is committing adultery."

"Ben's wife was unfaithful, Dad."

"I'm sorry to hear that, but be careful. You don't know what caused her to be unfaithful, and it breaks God heart whenever a divorce happens. It's not what He intended."

She held her father's gaze but her heart was in a jumble. Maybe it was all too hard and she should forget about Ben while she could. *But could she?* She bit her lip and looked away.

"Tell us about his son, Tessa," her mother said, touching her wrist lightly. "How old is he?"

Blinking, Tessa turned her head back. "He's just turned thirteen." She held her breath.

"Thirteen!" her father repeated. "Then this Mr.... *what's his name?* must be quite a few years older than you."

"His name is Ben, and no, not by much. He's only thirty-six."

"Must have had kids young, then."

"He only has one son. And we're only friends."

"So you say."

"I'm not as worried about Ben as I am about his son," her mother said. "If you two did become more than friends, have you thought what that would mean?"

Tessa tilted her head and looked at her mother, her brows pinched.

"If it got serious and he asked you to marry him, for example, you'd become an instant mother to a teenager. Raising a toddler's difficult enough, but a teenager? Are you ready for that?"

Tessa drew a sober breath. Put that way, maybe not. *Mother to a teenager?* "I doubt that would happen, and if it did, I'd pray long and hard about it." That would keep them happy. They both seemed to relax a little. "I know you're both looking out for me, but I don't think you should judge someone you've never met."

Her parents sat quietly for a minute.

"You're right," her father finally said. "The Bible tells us not to judge. Maybe we should meet this Ben before saying anything further. Even if he is *only a friend*."

"Why don't you invite him to dinner at our place?" Her mother smiled warmly. "Friday evening would suit."

"Really?" Tessa looked from one parent to the other. They really weren't that bad after all. "That would be wonderful. I'll ask both him and Jayden, that's his son, to come. Is that okay?"

"Of course, dear," her mother replied. "I have a soft spot for thirteen-year old boys."

Yes! Of course! Her mother had taken the young teens' class at church for years when she'd been younger.

The rest of the meal passed pleasantly, and on the way out, Tessa gave the ship's bell a double ring.

CHAPTER 14

he elevator doors slid nosily together. While this was only Ben's sixth week meeting with Stephanie, it seemed like he was heading up to the fourth floor office for the hundredth time. He'd thought about asking for a new counsellor, but in the end had decided to remain with her. She meant well, and maybe the connection with Tess would help, but he looked forward to the day when Stephanie would write him a clean bill of mental and emotional health and he'd no longer have any need to see her.

He knocked on the door and took a deep breath. If he was nervous, how must she be feeling? Finding out she'd set him up with Tess had shocked him. He could so easily have reported her.

She welcomed him in and asked how he was a little too quickly.

"You should know, Ms. Trejo. I suspect Tess has told you everything?"

"No. Not a word," she replied as she twiddled her pencil.

He sat in his regular chair and looked out the window. Fancy that. He felt sure Tess would have told her. His heart warmed at the thought of her. He should have returned her calls. Truth was, after fleeing the Pro-Am, he couldn't face anyone. In the end, he hadn't even gone to church, but instead stayed home and played computer games with Jayden. He'd even called in sick at work. No way could he face his colleagues. They would have seen photos of Kathryn with Luke in the newspaper, and he couldn't cope with that.

He must be the laughing stock of town. How many people knew about Kathryn and Luke but hadn't told him? *How could he have not known?*

"Most counselling sessions last for about two months, so we only have two more weeks unless you want to extend," Stephanie said, putting her pencil down. "Mr. Williams, do you think we could make a fresh start? I'm sorry. Disclosing your personal information, even to Tessa, was a mistake."

He sighed deeply. Maybe they could. He had to talk to someone—it may as well be her. He lifted his head. "Call me Ben. Please. It's time we were on first-name terms."

She visibly relaxed. "Ben, it is. Please call me Stephanie."

"Stephanie." He held her eyes and saw a young woman who cared. He'd never noticed that before, but maybe he hadn't been looking.

"Okay, let's make a start." She gave him an engaging grin.

By the end of the session, he had a new perspective on the grief she told him he'd been experiencing. When he let her do her job, Stephanie displayed wisdom beyond her years. He was happy to allow her to help him understand better the various stages of grief he'd been going through. He was still at Stage Three—*Anger*. Anger not so much that Kathryn had left—he'd basically dealt with that, but more directed at *how* she left and the fact that she showed no care or concern for how it impacted Jayden.

He still had four stages to go. *Four!* He pressed Stephanie to tell him what they were and how long it would take to get through them.

"In our next meeting, Ben. We've gone over enough right now. Of course, the stage I want you to arrive at is the seventh and last stage, which is one of acceptance and hope. I want to see you accept the past, but also be hopeful about your future. To get to that stage, though, you need to deal with your anger by forgiving Kathryn for her actions."

"*Forgive her?* You've got to be joking."

"Ben, you're a Christian. You need to forgive, just as Jesus forgave you. You're not there yet, but I don't think it'll be long. I can see God working in your heart."

He was silent. She had a point. "I guess I haven't got past my anger yet, so maybe you're right." Yes, he was a Christian. And forgiveness was a fundamental element of allowing God to work in his life. *But not yet.*

He left the meeting with a lighter step and with more determination than ever to be the father that Jayden needed. He'd think about forgiving Kathryn later.

TESSA TOUCHED up her lipstick and hair in the car mirror as soon as she pulled into Ben's driveway. She checked her lips once more in the front door window before ringing the bell. Her heart thumped as she waited. No-one answered.

She waited a full minute before ringing the bell again. Still no answer.

Guess I'll just have to try phoning again. But he hadn't returned any of her calls or texts, apart from saying he'd be in touch soon, so trying again probably wouldn't work. Maybe she'd just have to tell her parents he wouldn't be coming to dinner after all. She was about to leave when the door opened and Jayden stuck his head out. Hard rock music blasted through the house.

He eyed her up and down. "What do you want?"

"Hi Jayden. How are you?" *Silly question.* She bit her lip.

"Fine."

Her mother's words rang in her ears. *'Mother to a teenager...'* Maybe she was right. "That's good to hear. Is your dad home?"

He looked her up and down again. Maybe she should have changed out of her work clothes. "No, he isn't. He went to see his social worker ages ago."

She swallowed the lump that suddenly appeared in her throat. *I wonder how that's going...*

"You can wait if you want."

That's a surprise. More than one word.

"Thanks, but no, it's not necessary. Just tell your dad I'll phone later."

"Okay."

She'd just reached the bottom step when she remembered to ask about Bindy. She stopped and turned around. "Sorry Jayden, I meant to ask how Bindy was."

His face lit up. "She's good. Do you wanna see her?" He disappeared into the house before she could answer.

In a matter of moments, he was back with Bindy in his arms. He ran down the front steps and placed the dog on the ground in front of her. As she bent down to pat the puppy, Bindy stuck out a pink tongue and licked her hands, tickling her. She laughed. "She won't be a puppy much longer. She's getting so big."

"I'm trying to teach her some tricks. Wanna see?"

"That would be great."

"Jay, who are talking to?" They both looked toward the house, to where the gruff voice came from. A youth, quite a bit older than Jayden, stood inside the open front door. His blonde hair was in an undercut and a vine tattoo wrapped around his wrist.

"Just a friend of Dad's," Jayden replied before turning to Tessa. "That's Owen. His brother's one of my classmates. Gotta go. I'll show you Bindy's tricks another time."

"Don't forget to tell your Dad I'll call him." she said as she waved goodbye.

"I won't."

WHEN TESSA MADE her phone call to Ben later that evening, she prayed that this time he'd answer. She hadn't quizzed Stephanie about their meeting, nor had Stephanie volunteered any information, but from her cheeriness, Tessa guessed it had gone better than expected.

She hadn't spoken to Ben since he'd dropped her off after the Pro-Am. Now she felt awkward calling to ask him to dinner at her parents' house. Would he think it too forward and presumptuous? Probably. Maybe she should cancel it. Her parents might be happier if she did. She was just about to hit the cancel button when he answered. The sound of his deep voice made her knees go weak. Would she ever tire of listening to it? But now he'd finally answered, she could hardly speak.

So much had happened between them already, but she barely knew him. She'd read the passage about divorce in Matthew 19 like her father had suggested, and prayed about him as Pastor Stanek had said. She was trying to find out what made him tick, but whenever she was with him, she felt instantly happier. Something had clicked between them, and it wasn't just physical. Somehow they'd connected. But was that enough to invite him and his teenage son to dinner at her parents' place, especially when they were only friends? *And especially when he was divorced...*

His voice brought her back to the moment.

"Tessa, are you all right?"

"Sorry, I was miles away. How are you?" She slowed her breathing and prayed she'd say the right thing.

"I'm okay. Jayden said you came around this afternoon. I'm sorry I didn't return your calls."

"No problem. You had other things on your mind. I just wanted to see how you and Jayden were after what happened on Saturday. And I wanted to ask you something." There, she'd said it. Too late to change her mind now.

"We're doing all right. I'm hoping to have a good talk with him sometime soon. Maybe even tonight if his friends ever leave. Can you pray about it for me? I really don't know how to get him to open up. The only thing he ever wants to talk about is Bindy, but now, after seeing Kathryn..."

"Yes Ben, I'll pray." *I haven't stopped praying.*

"What did you want to ask?" His voice had softened and she pictured him sitting in his living room, his long legs stretched out in front of him, possibly resting his head on a cushion as he spoke to her. Her heart fluttered.

"Oh Ben, I'm embarrassed. Please tell me if this isn't appropriate."

"Sounds intriguing. Go on..."

She gulped nervously and took a deep breath. "When I had dinner with my parents the other night, my mother guessed I was seeing someone new. I said we were just friends, which we are, aren't we?" She didn't wait for an answer. "But anyway, they've invited you and Jayden over to their place for dinner on Friday night."

The silence on the other end of the line was deafening. Seconds ticked by. Her heart raced. Why wasn't he saying something? What was he thinking? What a fool she'd made of herself.

He finally answered. "You've taken me by surprise, I'll have to admit. But why not?" She let go of her breath. "Jayden's team isn't playing this Friday." She bit her lip. She'd forgotten about Jayden's football match. "And I've got nothing on, so yes, we'd be pleased to accept."

She felt like jumping for joy, but instead said she'd look forward to seeing him at puppy training on Thursday. And that she'd pray for his talk with Jayden.

CHAPTER 15

The week dragged and Friday came slowly. They hadn't much time to talk at puppy training, other than for Ben to quickly tell Tessa that his talk with Jayden had gone reasonably well but they still had a long way to go, and for her to give him the details for the following evening.

She chose a light blue summer dress to wear to dinner and had grabbed a light cotton cardigan in case the evening grew cool. She'd pulled her hair up in a loose bun—it was way too hot to leave down. After being stuck in khaki shorts most of the week, she was actually enjoying wearing a dress. It made her feel feminine, and blue suited her, so she'd been told.

She set the table for six at her parents' house while her mother put the food into serving dishes. Elliott's motorcycle roared and then died as he pulled into the driveway, and within minutes he appeared in the kitchen.

"Hi Mother." He bent down and gave her a kiss. "Whatever you're cooking sure smells good."

"Hands off." She tapped his hand as he reached for a warm bread roll, fresh from the oven. "Tonight's dinner is for Tessa's friend."

"Ah, yes! I nearly forgot. I should get ready."

"You should. And make it quick. They'll be here any minute."

"Hey, sis," he said as he passed through the dining room on the way to his bedroom. "I can't wait to meet Ben tonight, but you never told me what happened with you and Michael."

"Not now. I can't think about him right now."

"Never liked him anyway. He wasn't right for you."

Tessa straightened and faced her brother. "I don't need to be told that again." She kept her voice low so their mother wouldn't hear. "He had drug problems, and we broke up, okay? I haven't seen or heard from him for months, and I don't want to. You won't mention him at dinner, will you?"

He drew a finger across his lips. "My lips are sealed."

TESSA JUMPED when the doorbell rang although she'd been expecting it, having checked the clock in the kitchen every minute for the past half hour. Ben and Jayden arrived promptly at six, as she knew they would. She drew in a long breath to steady her nerves and called out that she'd get it.

She opened the door slowly. Her heart pounded. She'd never felt this way with Michael. It must be what true love felt like. Ben was dressed in dark casual slacks and a crisp, off-white button-down shirt, open at the collar. Such good dress sense. Even Jayden looked smart in his chinos and T-shirt. And he'd pinned his hair back from his face.

"Hello, Ben. Hello, Jayden." She smiled shyly as she stood before them, all of a sudden tongue-tied. Her eyes locked with Ben's and then everything happened in slow motion. Leaning forward, he kissed her on the cheek. The brush of his hand on her wrist sent a tingle through her body. Her breaths came faster. She had to stop this. She'd told her parents they were only friends.

She took a grip on herself. "Come in and meet my parents."

Her mother hurried from the kitchen and her father appeared from the living room. She introduced everybody.

Ben shook hands with her parents. Jayden followed suit, although he didn't look them in the eye. She tried to include him in the conversation, but he moved away and stood awkwardly on his own as the adults chatted about the weather, church, and business matters. A few minutes later, Elliott came down in a clean shirt and introductions were made all over again.

At the table, Ben sat beside her on one side and Jayden and Elliott sat across from them. Her parents sat at either end. After asking God to bless their food, her father and Ben started chatting about their careers, as she knew they would. Ben being an accountant was definitely a plus as far as her father was concerned. "Find someone with a good, steady occupation," he always used to say. Maybe that was one of the reasons he'd never liked Michael.

After the first course was finished, Tessa helped her mother clear the table. As she scraped and rinsed the dirty plates, her mother stacked the dishwasher.

"He's nice, Tessa." Her mother spoke quietly.

"Yes, he is." Tessa glanced back through the doorway. Ben

and her father were still deeply engrossed in conversation. Her heart warmed. Her father and Michael had rarely said more than two sentences to each other.

"But are you ready to throw your youth away?"

Tessa stopped scraping, taken aback at her mother's words. "What do you mean? We're only friends."

"Oh, Tessa. I can see the spark in your eyes. I noticed it the moment you arrived at dinner the other night, so don't tell me you're only friends."

She gulped. Only her mother would observe things like that. But they *were* only friends. Nothing had been said between them. They hadn't even held hands or kissed, but she couldn't deny that sitting beside him at her parents' table was doing strange things to her insides. She'd been very tempted to reach out and find his hand under the table or brush her leg against his.

"We *are* only friends. At the moment." Tessa looked into her mother's soft, caring eyes.

"Just don't do anything rash, dear. It would be such a big decision. Jayden seems a nice boy, but he'd be hard work." She gave Tessa a warm smile. "Here, take these bowls for dessert."

Tessa took the bowls and followed her mother into the dining room, the words still playing over in her mind when she reached the table. A loud clatter sounded. Everyone stopped what they were doing. Jayden had thrown his spoon across the table, hitting the glass bowl in the centre. "I don't want your religion stuffed down my throat," he shouted at Elliott before pushing his chair back and leaving the table in a huff.

Nobody dared move. Without thinking, Tessa placed her

free hand on Ben's shoulder. He stood, pushing his chair carefully back. "I'm sorry, please excuse me." He nodded his head apologetically to her parents and briefly met her gaze before he left the room and followed after Jayden.

"Whatever did you say to him, Elliott?" Tessa snapped at her brother, leaning forward.

Elliott's head hung low. "I was just trying to convince him that God loves him. I wasn't stuffing anything down his throat." His eyes blinked rapidly. "He believes God's an angry, Zeus-like figure who throws lightning bolts down from the sky to break up families."

"Jayden's really struggling at the moment. I know you meant well, but he's not ready." She drew a deep breath. This would set Jayden back even further.

"We're proud of your zeal, son, but you need to learn discernment." Their father tapped Elliott on the hand.

"I didn't think. I'm sorry." He spoke softly; his shoulders drooped. "I hope I haven't ruined the night."

"I hope not too." Tessa placed the bowls on the table. "I'll go check."

OUTSIDE, darkness was fast approaching; just the last lingering colours of sunset remained low on the horizon. Ben and Jayden stood on the driveway. Ben was speaking louder than Tessa had ever heard him speak, in fact, he was almost shouting, and he was throwing his hands around in the air. Jayden's body was hunched, his head hung low and his arms crossed. Why had Elliott been so thoughtless?

She joined them and stood beside Ben. "It's not Jayden's

fault, Ben. Elliott shouldn't have spoken to him like that. Don't take it out on Jayden, please."

Ben looked up. His face had reddened and he was breathing quickly.

"No. Jayden was a guest in your parents' house. He shouldn't have reacted like that."

"He's only a boy. Elliott should have known better. He's apologised."

She held Ben's gaze, surprised at her audacity. Is this what it would be like if they did become a couple? Maybe she wasn't ready after all. She felt she was taking sides already.

Her pulse raced as she waited. He finally tore his eyes away and directed his attention to Jayden.

"I'm disappointed in your behaviour, Jayden. Stomping out like that was the wrong thing to do. It was rude."

"Sorry." Jayden's arms remained crossed, but he lifted his head slightly.

"Well, that's a start." Ben's voice had lost some of its bite and she began to breathe easier.

"How about you come back in for dessert? Mum's baked a lemon cheesecake, and believe me, it's really delicious."

"I'll wait in the car until you're finished," Jayden said, turning away.

"Go ahead and wait," Ben said. "I'll have your slice."

Tessa placed her arm around Jayden's shoulder. "Come on, Jayden, come back in. It'll be all right. I've had words with my brother."

He shrugged without enthusiasm. "He'd better not talk to me about God again."

"I'll make sure of that, don't you worry."

They returned inside. Elliott apologised to Jayden. Jayden said he was sorry for stomping out like he did. The situation was diffused. But although her heart skittered when Ben reached for her hand under the table, Tessa began to wonder if she'd bitten off more than she could chew.

CHAPTER 16

The remainder of the evening at her parents' house passed uneventfully. Jayden loved her mother's baked lemon cheesecake so much that she wrapped the last piece for him to take home.

Tessa walked Ben and Jayden to their car after all the good-byes and thank-yous had been said with her parents and Elliott. When Jayden opened the front passenger door and climbed in, Ben grabbed her hand and pulled her close.

Her heart raced. This was the moment she'd been waiting for, but now it was here, she wondered if she'd let her feelings get in the way of rational thought. What would happen if he kissed her? Would it be the start of something she might not be able to stop, and might not want? It wouldn't be a casual relationship. They'd both be assuming it would lead to something more. Something permanent. She swallowed the lump in her throat. How would Jayden feel about that? Maybe he wasn't ready to share his dad with anyone else just yet. And maybe she wasn't prepared to deal with all the challenges they'd have to face. *God, what are You telling me?*

But he was so close, and his breath on her face was warm and sweet. Her heart pounded. He slipped his arm around her waist and drew her closer as he brushed some loose hair from her face with his finger.

"Thank you for tonight, Tess. And for stepping in with Jayden."

Every nerve in her body tingled as he studied her face. She wanted this so much, but as he lowered his lips to hers, she pulled away.

"I can't do this. I'm sorry." Her heart nearly broke. Was she really saying this?

He dropped his arm from her waist, but grabbed her hand before she moved out of reach.

"What's the matter, Tess? I thought you wanted this."

"I thought I did too. But I don't think I'm ready. I'm sorry." Her voice came out jagged, brittle.

He ran his hands over her hair with his other hand. "I'm sorry I rushed you. It was so difficult sitting beside you all night. It was all I could do to keep my eyes off you."

How could she turn him down? They both wanted each other, but something held her back. Did she really want to date a divorced man with a teenage son, even if she was madly attracted to him? She really didn't know.

"I need more time. I'm sorry." Her hands trembled as her heart fell apart. She took some deep breaths to steady herself.

He continued stroking her hair. She felt like grabbing his hand and kissing it. But she had to be strong and not let her feelings and desires take over, no matter how difficult that was.

She had to be sure. For once in her life she had to think before she acted.

"How about we spend more time talking and getting to know each other?"

Her body relaxed. *Yes. That's what's needed. Time.* She gazed into his eyes and saw understanding. "That would be great. Thank you. And I'm sorry, I really am." Her voice was faint but had lost its brittleness.

"It's fine. Really. I let my feelings get the better of me." His warm hand rested on the side of her cheek. "I want to get to know everything about you, but there's no hurry." His soft eyes caressed her face, and she almost gave in and kissed him. "How about we spend tomorrow together if you're free?'

Warmth spread through her body. "That would be lovely."

He leaned forward and placed a slow, tender kiss on her cheek. A promise of things to come.

AFTER HE AND JAYDEN LEFT, Tessa walked slowly back towards the house, in no hurry to return inside. No doubt she'd face a barrage of questions. Her parents and brother would want to talk about them for sure. *And whether she and Ben were more than friends.*

The warmth of the day lingered in the night air as she breathed in the heady fragrance of the frangipani flowers. This night would be etched in her memory forever. The night she turned down Ben's kiss. She stopped and leaned against the trunk of the huge leopard tree she'd helped her dad plant when she was only about nine. She slid down and sat on the grass below it and let out a huge sigh.

"Oh God, what have I got myself into? I can't believe that I turned Ben down. You know how much I like him, but I need guidance, direction. I don't know if I'm ready to be an instant mother. And I still don't know about the divorce issue. Please help me. You know I want to do the right thing, and I thank You for helping me to be strong and not act rashly. Thanks for helping Ben to understand. Please help us work through this. And God, please be with Jayden. Let him know You really do exist and that You love him to bits. Thank You, in Jesus' precious name, Amen."

The sound of dishes being washed and put away filtered through to the living area as she entered the house. Her parents were no doubt talking about Ben. She took a deep breath and joined them.

"Ah, Tess. There you are." Her father smiled warmly and held out his arms. She allowed him to pull her close and hug her. He kissed the top of her head before releasing her.

"That was a lovely evening, thank you both for everything."

Her mother dried her hands and turned around. "Our pleasure, honey. Cup of tea?" *The cue for 'let's have a chat'...*

"Sure."

Elliott joined them in the living room while her mother made tea for everyone. She didn't have to wait long for it to start.

"Well, that went off well, apart from that one little hiccup. I'm sorry about that, sis."

"It's okay. All is forgiven."

"But the kid's got some problems, you've got to agree?"

"Yes, but he's been through a lot. He's a good kid, and he'll come through it, eventually. We've just got to pray and trust God to work in his life."

"I like Ben," her father said, joining in. "For one, he's a Christian, and he's very well established in his career."

"Thought you'd like that." She gave him a wink.

"Yes, and he's stable, and he's serious. Seems like an honest person trying to do the right thing."

"I like his patience," her mother said, carrying a tray with four mugs of steaming hot tea into the room. "He handled the incident with his son very well, I thought."

"You're all talking as if we're about to get married. We're not even going out. We're just friends." She glanced at her mother. Would she say anything to the contrary?

"Yeah, yeah," Elliott said. "Tell us another one, sis."

"It's true. We're just friends." Tessa glared at him.

"Me thinketh the lady protests too much." He guffawed.

"Anyway," her father said, "I think we all approve. Much better than... what was his name?" He looked to her with a puzzled look on his face. "I always forget."

"Michael. His name was Michael."

"Ah yes, that's right. Well anyway, Ben's a much better choice."

"I guess that means you don't have an issue with him being divorced anymore? Not that it matters at the moment."

Her parents exchanged glances.

"About that," her mother said. "Your father and I need to tell you something we should have told you ages ago."

"Is this a cue for me to leave?" Elliott asked.

"No, you can stay," her mother said. "Both of you need to hear this." She moved to her husband's side and took his hand.

Moments passed. Tessa glanced at Elliott. He looked as puzzled as she felt. What secret were their parents about to divulge? She could hardly imagine her conservative parents having done anything they might be ashamed of enough to have kept hidden until now. *Maybe I'm illegitimate?* Wow! That would be a shock. But she'd seen their marriage certificate. She'd been born twelve months after their wedding. So no, it couldn't be that.

Their mother cleared her throat. Tessa and Elliott leaned forward.

"I know you think your dad is the only man I've ever been married to, but he's not."

Tessa's jaw dropped. *What? Mum's been married to someone else? No!*

"I was married once before. His name was Hugh." Dad took Mum's hand and squeezed it; she shot him a thankful smile. "We met in high school and we married when I was eighteen. My parents warned me against it, and I should have listened, but I loved him, and he loved me. At least, I thought he did. He was always considerate and promised to take care of me.

"Shortly after our wedding, his behaviour changed. He became abusive. Nothing I did, nothing I said pleased him anymore. He said I breathed too loudly. My body was ugly. He questioned my choice of clothing. He criticized my cooking and berated me when it didn't turn out as good as his mother's. Hardly a day went by when he didn't call me worthless or stupid." She paused to dab her eyes with a napkin from the table.

Tessa glanced at Elliott again, but her brother looked just as jarred as she felt. They'd never known their mother to cry—she'd always been calm, composed, and collected, no matter the circumstance. But now the woman they'd long admired for her quiet strength was opening up and showing another side they'd never seen—a more vulnerable side.

"At first, it was only verbal abuse," she continued. "But then it turned physical. He punched me and tried choking me. I wanted to leave, but I was too scared to tell anyone, even my own parents, what was happening. When I threatened to leave, he started to lock me in and refused to let me visit family or friends.

"I finally managed to speak to our pastor about what was happening, but instead of confronting Hugh about his behaviour, he blamed me for it. The pastor told me to submit to my husband as the Bible commanded, and things would get better. But they didn't. In fact, they got worse. I became depressed, and I hate to admit this, but I repeatedly begged God to end my life."

Tears streamed down her face. Tessa's eyes watered. Poor Mum. Why hadn't she and Elliott heard about this before?

Her mother pulled a tissue from her pocket and wiped her face. "When I wasn't begging God to end my life, I was begging Him to save my marriage. But I wanted out. I wanted to leave him, but my pastor told me that getting a divorce would be direct disobedience to God. Of course, I didn't want to go against God, so I kept praying for Him to fix it. But one day while praying, I clearly heard Him say it was okay to leave. So I did. I left Hugh. But for a long time afterwards, I felt I'd failed."

Dad hugged her and kissed the top of her head. She gave him a watery smile before continuing.

"When I moved here to Brisbane, I started going to Grace-pointe Church. That's where Pastor Stanek told me that God didn't love me any less because I'd left Hugh. He told me that

God doesn't condone any man who berates and beats a woman, and that He'd never expect the woman to stay. Even though it's not what He intended, in some circumstances, leaving is the only option. Only when I heard that did I finally experience complete and total freedom from the pain of that failed marriage. I was finally able to forgive myself."

"Mum, I'm so sorry." Tessa moved to the seat beside her mother and hugged her.

"You needn't be," she said, a faint smile appearing on her tear-stained face. "Leaving Hugh was the second best decision I've made."

"What was the first?" Elliott asked.

"Marrying your father," she replied, turning to smile lovingly at him. "After such a horrible first marriage, I was very hesitant about getting involved with someone again, but now I can't imagine life without your dad."

"And I can't imagine what my life would have been like without you, Ellie. I'm glad you decided to give love another chance. I know we... well, me especially, sounded rather harsh about Ben being divorced the other day when we were at dinner. Because of what the Bible says, I still believe divorce is wrong in most situations. It's not what God intends for us at all. He intends marriage to be a lifetime commitment, and if we lived in a perfect world, there'd be no need for divorce, but we don't live in a perfect world, and in situations like your mother found herself in, divorce really was the only option.

"We don't know what happened in Ben's marriage, and what caused his wife to be unfaithful, but I can't imagine he was a wife beater. She must have had her own reasons, which we might never know." He paused and squeezed Tessa's hand.

"What we're trying to say is, if you and Ben do eventually become more than friends, we'll be okay with it, but don't make any hasty decisions. Get to know him first before making any long-term decisions. And pray about it. Really pray. You need to know what's in his heart. Only God can show you that. And you also should talk with Pastor Stanek. It's a serious thing, and you need to be sure that whatever you decide is in line with God's will."

Tessa blinked back tears. She couldn't have asked for more caring, understanding, and wise parents. She was blessed indeed.

CHAPTER 17

*T*essa was finishing breakfast the following morning when Ben telephoned. He arranged to pick her up within the hour and suggested they drive to the Gold Coast and spend the day at the beach.

"That sounds wonderful. I'll look forward to seeing you soon."

"I won't ask," Stephanie said as she collected the dishes, "but it sounds like you two are hitting it off."

"We're friends. That's all."

Stephanie gave her a knowing look and placed the dishes in the sink. "Okay, I won't say any more. I just hope you know what you're doing."

"We're just going to the beach. That's all. And I need to get ready."

Half an hour later, Tessa pulled the curtains back and peeked out the window when the gate squeaked open.

"I'm off, Steph." She grabbed her bag and hat and ran down

the stairs. She resisted the temptation to give Ben a hug and instead greeted him with a beaming smile. He looked so... appealing. But she knew what he looked like on the outside— today was all about getting to know what made him tick on the inside.

"Such a lovely day for the beach. Good suggestion." She laughed lightly and walked beside him to the car. Jayden sat in the back, playing on his iPad. She berated herself for not even thinking about whether Jayden would be coming or not.

"Good morning, Jayden. How are you?"

He lifted his head and grunted before returning to his iPad.

"Would you like to sit in the front?"

He shook his head.

She shot Ben a questioning look. He held her gaze and answered her question with his eyes. Things still weren't crash hot between them. Sliding into the front seat, she felt she was gatecrashing again. Was this a foolish decision? Maybe she should have told him it wasn't going to work and left it at that. But she couldn't deny the attraction between them. And maybe, just maybe they could work through everything else.

"So, Ms. Scott, what are we going to talk about?" He asked as he put the car into drive and pulled away from the kerb.

"Oh, I don't know. You pick."

"Okay then, why did you decide to become a vet?"

For the whole hour and a bit it took to get to the coast, they chatted easily, discovering each other's likes and dislikes, tastes in food, what their childhoods were like, what their favourite holiday destinations were, in fact, almost everything.

Jayden seemed happy enough to be at the beach. He'd brought his body-board and caught wave after wave with Ben while Tessa enjoyed swimming in the clear blue water. The surf was calm, the conditions perfect. The beach was packed with people trying to escape the heat of late summer, but even still, once they moved away from the main swimming area, they almost felt like they were on their own.

It was later, when they were walking along Surfers Paradise with Jayden dragging behind again, that they talked about their faith. "So, how did you become a Christian?" Tessa glanced at the man walking beside her. His quiet sincere manner impressed her so much.

"After Dad died, Mum started going to church again. She used to go when she was young, but when she got married and Dad didn't go, she stopped as well." He paused and took a deep breath. "I think she would have loved to keep going, but she was fairly timid in those days, and she didn't go against what Dad said. But once he was no longer around, she grabbed the opportunity. She made new friends and became a much happier person almost overnight."

He paused again and looked at Tessa. "I'm not saying she didn't miss Dad, but her life with him wasn't that great." He returned his gaze to the endless white sand stretching out in front of them. "She got involved in church activities and encouraged me to go to the evening services with her. I'd hardly been to church so I didn't know what to expect, but the number of people amazed me. I guess I'd expected just a handful of oldies, but there were hundreds, and many of them were young.

"I was at that point in my life when I was searching for something, so after I'd heard the gospel message a few times, I started reading the Bible, as well as books on Apologetics. I couldn't just follow blindly—I had to have some solid proof that God actually existed and that Jesus was a real person. I also spent a lot of time in study groups, and finally it all made sense and I gave my heart to the Lord. I guess it wasn't as emotional as some conversions, but I suppose that's me. It doesn't mean I wasn't grateful for everything Jesus had done for me—I was just a little more reserved. But I know deep down that when I gave my heart, God did something inside me I couldn't explain. My walk since then has been steady and normal, that was, until the day Kathryn walked out."

"Where did you meet her?"

"At church. She started coming with a bunch of girlfriends. I think in hindsight she only came because they told her there were a lot of guys there. I remembered her from school, and we hit it off, but I think she chased me more than I chased her. She gave her heart to the Lord just like everybody did back then, but later I wondered if she really understood what she'd done. Her faith, now I think of it, was quite shallow. She was always asking God to give her things. I can't remember her ever thanking Him for saving her."

The sun dropped behind a tall building, casting a long shadow on the beach. Tessa shivered.

Ben glanced at his watch. "Look at the time. How did that go so quickly?"

"Guess it's the old saying, *time flies when you're having fun*." She laughed lightly and flashed him a playful smile.

"You're probably right. Shall we head back?"

"A pity to leave, but I guess so."

"How about we grab fish and chips on the way home?"

"Sounds great. I'm not in a hurry to get back."

By the time they'd eaten dinner and driven back to Tessa's cottage, darkness was falling on the city. Having spent most of the day talking, on the way home they listened to Chris Tomlins's latest album, much to Jayden's annoyance. He stuck his earplugs in.

"Thank you for a lovely day, Ben." She reached out and squeezed his hand. The whole day they'd avoided touching each other apart from when they'd rubbed suntan lotion onto each other's backs, but now his warm hand was in hers, she struggled to let go. Her flesh tingled as he returned her squeeze and gazed into her eyes.

"Let's do it again, and soon." He leaned forward and kissed her cheek.

She closed her eyes as his lips lingered on her skin. "Yes, let's."

CHAPTER 18

$\mathcal{T}$he next morning, Ben sat quietly reading his Bible at the kitchen table while Jayden prepared breakfast. Ben had been surprised but pleased when he'd offered to cook, and now the mouth-watering aroma of toasted waffles and freshly brewed coffee mingled in the air.

"Do you want whipped cream with your waffles?" Jayden asked as he put two lumps of sugar into Ben's favourite mug and began stirring.

"No, just syrup, thanks." Ben closed his Bible and set it aside.

"We've only got triple berry fruit syrup."

"That's fine. I take it you grew tired of my cooking." Ben raised his brow and grinned playfully as Jayden set two plates on the table. "I don't blame you. I'm not much of a chef."

Jayden rolled his eyes. "No offense, Dad, but you're not even a little bit of a chef. Nearly everything you make tastes like cardboard. Maybe you should ask Tessa's mum to teach you to cook. Dinner at their house was the first time we've had a proper home-cooked meal in forever."

"Maybe I will."

"Are you going to ask Tessa to marry you?" Jayden's eyes narrowed. "I saw you kiss her."

"I do like her. But no, we're just friends. But what do you think of her?"

He shrugged, as if he didn't care. "Guess she's all right, but…" He stopped short and lowered his eyes.

"It's okay, son. Nothing's going to change in a hurry. Anyway, we'd better get ready for church."

"I don't want to go."

"Why not?"

"Just don't like going. It's boring and I've got better things to do. Seems like a waste of time."

"I remember feeling like that myself when I was young. Sometimes I still do." Ben placed his mug on the table. "If I were honest, I'd probably rather play a round of golf or take the boat out for a sail, but I believe that going to church and worshipping God with other believers is more important. I know it's hard to understand, especially at your age, but it's important. Real important."

Jayden slunk back in his chair and crossed his arms.

Ben's heart ached for him. It'd be so easy to let him stay home, but if he did, that would just be the start. No, he couldn't give in. "Come on, Jayden. Don't make it difficult. I'll clear the dishes while you get ready."

Jayden shot him a filthy look, but stood and dragged himself up the stairs.

THEY SLIPPED into a back pew of the church. After a few songs, Pastor Petersen stood up to preach. It seemed fitting that his sermon was about new beginnings. Ben prayed God would speak directly into Jayden's heart, but Jayden sat low in the pew with his arms crossed. Strange he'd chosen to stay in church and not go to the youth program. But was he listening?

The Scripture passage Pastor Petersen read from was Isaiah 43:18-19: *"Forget the former things; do not dwell on the past. See, I am doing a new thing! Now it springs up; do you not perceive it? I am making a way in the wilderness and streams in the wasteland."*

He closed the Bible and looked out at the congregation. "Isaiah wrote this to the children of Israel when they were going through a dark and difficult time. They'd lost everything, they'd been removed from their own homes, and they were in captivity in a strange land. God wanted to do a new thing with the children of Israel then, but what now?" He paused, casting his gaze around the congregation. "Maybe you're going through a difficult season. If so, be assured that God wants to do a new thing in your life too. But to accept the new thing God wants to do, you must stop looking behind and start looking ahead."

Ben touched the indent on his ring finger, a constant reminder of the past. If he could, he would remove it in an instant.

"You can't allow past victories to validate you. You can't allow past failures to define you. God says to 'forget the former things; do not dwell on the past'. He doesn't condemn you for the negative things in your past. You can't do anything to change them. Instead, God offers hope and forgiveness, and a fresh chance to start over."

"Amen," Ben said quietly. It was just as Stephanie had told him to do in their last meeting: leave the past in the past, accept the present, and look forward to the future. Kathryn was part of his past, and he was now convinced God wanted to do a new thing in his life. He couldn't help but wonder if Tessa was part of that new thing.

"A second thing you must do is to start seeing yourself as God sees you. Perhaps you've lost your job, perhaps your marriage isn't what it should be, perhaps you're struggling financially. You may feel that God is disappointed in you, but He's not. You may feel that God doesn't want to have anything to do with you, but nothing could be further from the truth. Romans 8:1 says there is no condemnation for those who are in Christ Jesus."

Ben felt the Lord touching his heart. Yes, he had thought God was disappointed in him. He thought he'd failed and had let Him down.

"The third thing you must do is to commit, or recommit, yourself to Him. God won't force His new thing on you. If you refuse His offer of a fresh chance, then your life will remain a wasteland. God has a wonderful plan for your life. Will you choose to follow Him?"

As the pastor prayed aloud over the entire congregation, Ben bowed his head and talked silently to God, promising to do just that. He asked God to give him the faith and courage to love and trust again. *And to forgive.*

The last song was the old hymn *It Is Well with My Soul.* The tune stayed with Ben on his drive back home. He thought about the lyrics over and over again. After a long period of agitation and restlessness over Kathryn's leaving, peace like a river finally came his way. He didn't know what was ahead, but whatever the future held, it was well with his soul. Glancing at Jayden, he prayed it would be well with his son's soul too.

CHAPTER 19

"*O*ur last meeting!" Stephanie said as Ben entered her office a week and a bit later.

"I don't mean to be rude, but I'm glad, actually." He lowered himself into the armchair opposite her desk and glanced at the drawn blinds.

She followed his gaze. "I don't care for wet, grey days."

He turned to face her. "I'm glad this is it. Not because I don't want to see you. But I do believe I've worked through my issues and I'm good to go."

"I'm so glad to hear that," she said, smiling warmly. "But before we finish up, let's recap so you can fully appreciate the progress you've made. It'll also help me do my final report." She clicked her pen and winked at him. "When you first came in, you were closed and depressed. And lonely. You were grieving, but didn't know it. You were angry and bitter, and confused. Basically, you were showing almost all the initial stages of grief at the same time."

"And I was on antidepressants."

"Yes, you were." She leaned back in her chair and looked at him thoughtfully. "I'm guessing you're not on them anymore?"

"No. Stopped taking them a couple of weeks ago."

"That's good to hear. Much better not to take them if you don't need to. So, I think you're at Stages six and seven of the grief process, but I'd like to go through the middle stages with you before we talk about exactly where you're at if you don't mind."

Ben leaned forward. "Do we have to? I'd really like to move on if we can. Just this past week I've had some major break-throughs, and I'd prefer to talk about them rather than rehash things that aren't relevant anymore."

"I'm sorry. I was just following procedures. By all means, please tell me what's happened. I'd love to hear." She placed her pen on the desk and closed her notebook. "I'm all ears. Over to you."

He took a slow breath and sat back in his chair. He glanced at the drawn blinds. "Do you mind if we open them? I'd rather see the sky, even if it's grey."

"Sure. No problem." She stood and opened the blinds, revealing dark grey storm clouds. Flashes of lightning split the sky in the distance, and at any moment the clouds could open and release the torrential rain that had been forecast.

Ben stared out at the sky for a moment and allowed his mind to steady. Where should he start? So much had happened over the past couple of weeks. This was almost more for his own benefit than Stephanie's. But having her here in front of him would make him verbalise the feelings in his heart, and he needed to do that. To put some order into the myriad of thoughts and feelings that had been swirling around over the past weeks. He turned his head and cleared his throat.

"When Kathryn and I married, I took our wedding vows very seriously. I'd never thought the day would come when those vows would mean nothing. Finding out she was with that golfer confirmed I'd failed her. She obviously needed more attention than I could give her." He paused and inhaled slowly. "When we first started going out, we used to do fun things together. I even surprised her with a trip to Paris not long after we were married. But when Jayden came along, I think I took the responsibility of being a father and a provider a little too seriously, and rather than focusing on being there to support her physically and emotionally, I concentrated on supporting her financially and ended up spending too much time at work."

They both jumped as a clap of thunder boomed outside.

"Sorry. Where was I? Oh, that's right… I obviously missed all the cues that she was unhappy. She didn't want any more children. I thought it was because she'd had such a difficult pregnancy, but now I think it was because she didn't want to be tied down to what she perceived to be a normal boring life. Maybe if I'd been more aware I could have changed things." He paused and looked out the window. "It was too late to do anything by the time she walked out."

He drew a deep breath and turned his head back. "The divorce no longer dominates my thoughts. I've gotten used to the fact that she's not coming back and I'll be living the rest of my life without her. Accepting that has lifted a great weight off my shoulders, if you know what I mean. There isn't any speculation about whether or not she's coming back. She isn't. And I no longer have anxiety about where she is or what she's doing. I do feel bad that I let her down, however."

Stephanie went to speak, but he lifted his hand.

"My main priority now is Jayden. A lot of people are surprised Kathryn didn't take him with her. To be honest, I don't know what I would have done if she had. He's my life, and I love him with all my heart. I just wish I could help him more. Occasionally he opens up a little and talks about it, but mainly he just holds it all in. Much like I did, I guess. I pray for him every day. And I pray that God will give me wisdom in dealing with him. The last thing I want is for him go off the rails, but I can't even imagine what he's feeling. I try to think how I would have felt if my own mother had just up and left without saying anything. It would be the hugest rejection. I try to show him how much I love him and how much he means to me every day, but I don't think it's enough. Bindy's helped, but even she isn't enough." Tears stung his eyes, and he looked away.

Stephanie leaned forward and handed him a tissue. "Jayden's lucky to have you as his dad." Her voice was soft and caring. "I'm sure he knows how much you love him and that you'll never let him down. But yes, I agree, he needs more than that. He needs to know God's love and healing power in his life. He would definitely still be feeling unloved and rejected by his mother, and it's such a hard age. Encourage him to talk to someone. I know he won't at the moment, but let's pray he will sometime soon."

"Yes." Ben drew a deep breath and steadied himself. "So, all of this leads me to the past week or so. I'd been struggling to hear God's voice through my anger and depression. After

Kathryn left, I kept going to church, but I wasn't really open to hearing from God, especially in the early days. I just wanted Him to bring her back. But recently I started to pray more than ever before. I guess because I knew deep down that only God could fix things properly, and I needed to hear from Him. My main prayer was for Him to give me peace to accept the things I couldn't change, and strength to be the best father I could be to Jayden." He paused and lifted his gaze. "These counselling sessions have helped me see that even when life doesn't turn out as planned, God can still work things out for good. I just need to be patient and learn to trust Him."

He took a breath and glanced out the window as rain started pelting against the glass, causing a deafening din. He spoke louder just to be heard. "Last Sunday at church, I recommitted my life to God, and I know He has a new thing planned for my life, and I'm really looking forward to it."

"That's wonderful." Stephanie's smile was genuine and warm. "We know that in all things God works for the good of those who love Him, who've been called according to His purpose." She leaned forward. "As a Christian Social Worker, one of my main goals is to help people realise the help and the hope that's available to all of us in God when we go through hard times."

She leaned back and crossed her arms. "I'm so glad, despite our rocky start, that our time together has helped." She raised her brows, a playful grin growing on her face before she readopted her professional manner. "When you first came into my office, I sensed you were full of self-doubt and were suffering from a poor self-image. I think you really believed you'd failed as a husband and as a father. But God doesn't condemn you."

Her voice softened, and her gaze settled on his. "Your worth as a man isn't in how good, or even in how bad, you consider yourself to be as a husband or father. Your worth is found in Christ, and in Him alone."

"Amen for that!" Ben's voice was lighter, as was his heart as he recalled Pastor Petersen's words; *'There's no condemnation for those in Christ Jesus.'*

Stephanie smiled broadly. "You seem so much more hopeful and positive, Ben. I really do wish you all the best. We've had some journey, haven't we? I have to say you tested me at the beginning, but I've learned a lot too, so thank you, Mr. Williams."

He stood and shook her hand. "Thank you too, Ms. Trejo." Ben's grin grew wide as the realization he'd finally reached the end of his formal sessions sank in. "I guess we can stop this formal stuff now and just be friends. We might be seeing more of each other from now on, anyway."

"Really? Are you and Tess formally dating?"

His grin expanded into a sheepish smile. "Not yet, but I'm hoping she'll agree when I see her this afternoon. We've spent this whole past week and a bit talking, and I think she might finally be ready to become more than just friends."

"I hope so. You two will make a great couple."

"And of course, you had no little hand in it yourself?"

She let out a small laugh and slapped him playfully on the back as she peered along the empty corridor. "Let's keep that a secret, shall we?"

He lifted his index finger to his lips. "My lips are sealed."

"Thank you. See you soon."

BEN STOPPED by Hungry Jack's to pick up burgers, fries, and sundaes for Jayden and his friends who'd come over again after school. He was waiting in the drive-thru for the order to be brought out when his phone rang. Jayden's friend, Neil, was on the other end, sounding hysterical. "Mr. Williams, something's wrong with Jayden."

"What do you mean, *something's wrong*?" Ben's heart raced. What could possibly have happened?

"I don't know. We were playing a game, and he just collapsed."

"What were you playing?" Ben put the phone on hands-free and pulled out of the drive-thru line and turned back out onto the road. Burgers were the last thing on his mind now. Jayden had been perfectly fine this morning.

Neil hadn't answered his last question.

"Neil, what were you playing?"

"We were just daring each other." Neil's voice had quieted.

Ben yanked the volume control up. "To do what?"

"We found some old pills and were trying to see who could take the most."

"You *what?*"

"I think he took too many."

"Okay, listen to me. Don't leave him. I'm almost home. I'll call the ambulance."

Ben hung up and dialled the emergency number, sending up a quick prayer as he waited. "God, I trust You, but please don't let my son die."

CHAPTER 20

*A*s Ben turned into the street, the ambulance was already parked in his driveway. Across the street, a neighbour he hardly knew had stopped clearing the storm debris from her front yard and stood on the footpath watching the scene.

"What's happened? I hope everything's all right," the woman called out as Ben jumped out of his car.

"My son had an accident," he answered hastily, not wanting to engage in conversation.

"Oh my! I hope he's not too bad."

"I hope so too." He gave her a dismissive nod and dashed to the porch steps where Neil and his seventeen-year-old brother, Owen, were being questioned by a woman paramedic holding a clipboard.

"Do you know what kind of drug he took?" the paramedic asked.

Neil shook his head. He was rocking back and forth and

sweat ran down his forehead.

"It was Serepax and something else," Owen said evenly, his eyes wide, staring at nothing.

"So he was taking two different kinds? Where did he get them from?"

"In the house," Owen replied.

"They were mine," Ben said as he approached. "I was taking Serepax and Norpramin for anxiety and depression. They were prescribed, but I should have thrown them away."

"Is Jayden going to be okay?" Neil asked. His face had turned white.

Just then, two other paramedics emerged from the house carrying Jayden on a stretcher. A breathing tube was in his mouth and covered his nose. His lips and fingertips were blue and the rest of his skin, pale.

Ben grabbed hold of his hand. Cold and limp. "Jayden, can you hear me? I'm right here."

He didn't respond.

"His heart beat has slowed considerably," the woman paramedic said. "He isn't in a coma, just unconscious right now. We need to get him to hospital as quickly as possible to have him treated properly."

"What about these two? Do they need to be checked out?" Ben pointed to the two boys still sitting on the step, staring into space.

"Yes, just in case. They seem okay, but you never know. We'll take them in the other ambulance. Their parents have been called."

The paramedics gently, but quickly, loaded Jayden into the back of the ambulance. Ben climbed in and sat beside him, holding his hand the whole way to the Wesley Hospital. The entire trip, he prayed that the drugs Jayden had taken wouldn't do any long-term damage to his body. He thought about whom to call and immediately sent a text message to Tessa asking her to pray.

Once at the hospital, Jayden was wheeled behind large double doors into an operating room. Ben wanted to follow, but he was directed to an almost empty waiting room.

"I know you're concerned, but there's nothing you can do at the moment, Mr. Williams," the woman paramedic said. "You'll be able to see him once he's resting in his room. Is there anything I can get you?"

"No, I'm fine." But he wasn't.

The paramedic brought him some water anyway. "Just in case." She set the paper cup and some napkins on a table. "Try to relax. Trust me, your son is in capable hands."

He forced a smile. Besides the receptionist behind a computer desk, he was the only one in the waiting room. He paced back and forth, watching the clock. After thirty minutes had passed, he sat down and tried praying again.

His mind wandered to what had happened in his house. Jayden knew better than to go around taking pills that didn't belong to him. He wasn't too worried about Neil. He and Jayden were the same age and had been best friends since their kindergarten years. He was funny and talkative, and Ben didn't mind them hanging together. It was Owen who concerned him. Four years older than the other two, Owen had dropped out of high school and had already been in trouble with the police for drinking and driving and selling illicit drugs to his former classmates.

Ben ran his hand through his hair and chastised himself. *I should have stopped Jayden from hanging around with him ages ago.* Once Jayden recovered, he'd talk to him about it, and he'd also talk to the boys' parents. Ben's brows came together. Strange they weren't here.

"BEN, is Jayden going to be okay?" Ben looked up at the sound of the familiar voice. Eleanor Scott was hurrying towards him; worry and concern filled her face. Telford and Tessa were close behind. Tessa carried a bunch of blue iris flowers and a *Get Well* card.

"We prayed as soon as Tessa told us what happened," Telford said, placing a hand on his shoulder. "Since we didn't hear back, we thought we'd come by to see if we could do anything to help."

"Where is he?" Tessa asked, quickly scanning the room.

"In the operating room. They said he should pull through, but he was still unconscious when he got here."

"He's a tough kid, I'm sure he'll be just fine," Telford said.

"Thanks." Ben gave Tessa's dad a weak smile. She and her mother both quizzed him about what had happened. He relayed all he knew. "I should have thrown those pills away." He let out a self-deprecating sigh and glanced at Tessa. "I wasn't using them anymore."

"Don't blame yourself." She sat down beside him. "No one could have foreseen this happening. Hopefully Jayden will learn a lesson."

"I hope so. I won't be letting him hang around Owen anymore, that's for sure. He's a bad influence." Ben glanced at the clock on the wall. Nearly two hours had passed since Jayden had been taken behind the large double doors he wasn't allowed to enter. *How much longer could it take?* He reached out and took Tessa's hands without even thinking what she or her parents would think. It was the most natural thing to do. Having her here made the waiting bearable.

The four adults sat and chatted in low tones about the general events of the day and about their families.

"Do your parents live nearby?" Eleanor asked.

"They used to, but both my parents have passed away."

"Oh, I'm sorry. I shouldn't have asked," she said, patting his hand lightly.

"It's okay. My dad died quite a while ago. He had a major heart attack. Totally unexpected. And my mum. Well, she had an accident a few years back and died from her injuries."

"That's so sad."

He let out a deep sigh. "Yes, but at least I know my mum went to a better place. I'm not so sure about my dad."

"It must be hard on Jayden not having any grandparents around."

"Yes, he cried for days when my mum died. Besides Kathryn, who isn't involved in his life anymore, I'm basically the only family he has."

Tessa gave his hand a squeeze. "And you're a great dad. Jayden couldn't ask for anyone better."

JUST THEN THE doctor came in, followed by a nurse, and they all looked up expectantly. The doctor stood for a moment in silence with his hands in the pockets of his long, white jacket.

"Anytime a person under the age of eighteen overdoses, we take it very seriously," he said gravely. "Mr. Williams, is your son unstable? Does he have a history of mental illness, bipolar disorder, or anything of the sort?"

"No, he's perfectly normal and healthy."

"Do you believe his overdose was a suicide attempt?"

Ben's head jerked up. *Suicide attempt?* "Absolutely not. He was playing a stupid game with some friends and things got out of hand. That's all."

"Is Jayden all right?" Tessa asked the doctor.

"I'm getting there, ma'am," he replied before turning his attention back to Ben. "We pumped your son's stomach and gave him some activated charcoal. He's conscious, but he's sleeping at the moment. When he wakes, he may still feel sick and weak, but those physical symptoms should be gone within a week."

Ben breathed easier at hearing this good news. Tessa took his hand and gave it another squeeze.

"We considered putting him on psychiatric hold, but as he doesn't have a history of mental illness and since you don't consider him suicidal, we'll only keep him overnight to monitor his stability. We expect to release him tomorrow morning."

"Can we see him now?"

"Yes, but as I said, he's sleeping, and it'd be best not to wake him."

"He's in Room 262," the nurse added. "I'll take you there."

"Thank you," Ben said, shaking the doctor's hand. Tessa picked up the flowers and card and they all followed the nurse to Jayden's room.

CHAPTER 21

The small hospital room was crammed with a bed, a chair and table, a closet, and several blinking, beeping medical machines. A television sat in the corner. As the doctor had advised, Jayden was asleep. Some of the colour had returned to his skin and his cheeks were flushed. An IV drip, hooked up to his arm, pumped clear liquid into his body. Ben went up to the bed and kissed the top of his head.

"Let me pray for him," Telford said. Ben nodded his agreement. The four adults gathered in a semi-circle around the bed and held hands with bowed heads. "Heavenly Father, we thank You for preserving Jayden's life. Heal him physically and heal him spiritually as well. Jayden's a good child, but his heart is prone to wander. Even though he hasn't yet believed in You, we know that He's Yours. Help us as his friends and family to help him through his confusion and pain. However, we can't save him. Only You can do that, and so we pray that You'll open his eyes and heart to Your love. Have him to come to You.

Draw his heart close to Yours and keep him safe in Your hands. In Your precious Son's name, Amen."

"Amen," they all repeated.

"Thank you." Ben's eyes blurred with tears. "And thank you all for coming, and for your support."

Eleanor hugged him. "It's the least we could do."

He smiled warmly at this woman he was coming to admire greatly. What a fine example of a godly Christian couple she and Telford were. He returned his attention to Jayden and brushed his cheek. What was he thinking, taking those tablets? Ben couldn't believe his son had been so stupid.

"He's looking okay." Tessa stood behind him, her voice soft and caring.

He nodded. "Yes, it looks like he'll pull through, thank the Lord." He turned and came face to face to her. Their eyes met briefly, and gratitude for her support, and that of her parents, warmed his heart. She shifted back, allowing him space to move.

"Have you eaten?" Eleanor asked.

"No. I was getting burgers when I got the call."

"Why don't you and Tessa get something to eat while Telford and I stay here with Jayden? We don't have any place important to go."

"Are you sure? I don't want to put you out any further."

"It's fine, and you're not putting us out," Telford said, glancing at his wife. "I'll grab another chair."

"Let me," Ben said, already heading out the room. He returned a moment later with another chair which he squeezed into the space at the end of Jayden's bed.

"It's been a challenging day for you, Ben. Take your time.

We'll call if Jayden wakes up or if there are any changes."
Telford squeezed his shoulder.

"Thank you, I appreciate it."

Ben ruffled Jayden's hair lightly as he placed another kiss
on his cheek. "Get well, son. I love you. I'll be back soon."

~

TESSA SUGGESTED they go to one of the restaurants on Park
Road, not far from the hospital. Ben agreed, and they drove the
short distance in her car. The popular dining street was lined
with an array of restaurants, and even though it was a Tuesday
night, most were bustling with diners enjoying the balmy late
summer evening.

They chose the French restaurant, *Rue de Paris*, tucked away
behind a small replica of the Eiffel Tower, and sat at a table
surrounded by lattice work covered in sweet jasmine and
wandering allamanda. Water from a large fountain in the
middle of the courtyard trickled down the figurine of a Roman
lady holding a basket of fruit. Soft music played in the
background.

"This is lovely, Ben. I haven't been here for a long time."

"Neither have I. I used to come here with Kathryn…"

Tessa touched his hand lightly. "I'm sorry, you should
have said."

"No. It's fine, it really is." He took her hand and stroked it
gently with his thumb. Her pulse quickened. They'd avoided
touching since the day at the beach, and now the feel of his
warm hand on hers stole her breath away.

"I've really enjoyed these past few weeks, getting to know

you and your family. Although I may never fully understand how or why Kathryn decided to leave not only me, but Jayden, I've forgiven her, and I'm ready to move on." His soft eyes gazing into hers melted her heart.

"Before I met you, I was depressed about the future, but now I'm full of hope, even with what's happened today." He paused and closed his eyes briefly.

She squeezed his hand. He must be feeling terrible about Jayden.

He opened his eyes and gave her a smile that grew from the corner of his lips as he threaded his fingers through hers. "Tess, I appreciate your kindness and concern for others. And I admire your devotion and faith in God. It inspires me to be more dedicated to my own faith." He paused again and held her gaze; his Adam's apple bobbed in his throat when he swallowed. "And these are just a few of the reasons I'm hoping you'll allow me to court you properly." He put a finger to her lips when she tried to speak. "Let me finish."

"I don't ask this lightly. I don't want to enter into a relationship without you being clear of my intentions. I wouldn't consider dating anyone if I couldn't see myself married to them. I thank God for bringing us together. Take as long as you need to think about it, but when I talked to you at that first puppy training class, I knew then that someone seriously special had just stepped into my life. I was, and still am, mesmerized by your laughter, and your enthusiasm for living."

She couldn't believe what she was hearing. Had he mentioned *marriage*, or had she misheard?

His grip on her hand tightened. "I know it's asking a lot, not only because I'm a divorcee, but because of Jayden. You'd be taking on a package deal, and I don't know how you feel about that, especially after today." He let out a slow breath as he held her gaze.

Her mother's words rang in her head: '..he'd be hard work...' She gulped.

"I don't want you to rush into making a decision, but know this, Tessa Scott, I'm falling in love with you, and I'm hoping you feel the same about me." He squeezed her hand gently. "Now you can speak."

His playful grin lightened the moment, but a hard lump had formed in her throat and she could barely speak. Over the past weeks she'd been asking herself and God those very same questions. Although he wasn't asking her to marry him, it was almost the same thing. If she agreed to let him court her, *how old fashioned was that?* She giggled at the thought of being courted, it would lead to marriage unless something unforeseen happened. Ben was the most loving and kind man she'd ever known, and having spoken at length with Pastor Stanek about the divorce issue, she had peace in her heart, and she could imagine herself married to Ben and sharing her life with him. Being a mum to Jayden would be a challenge, but with Ben by her side and God in her heart, she could face whatever that might entail. Her heart overflowed with love for him. Yes, she would allow Mr. Ben Williams to officially court her.

She took his hands in hers and smiled into his eyes. "Yes, I do feel the same about you, Ben, and yes, I'd love you to court me."

He leaned forward, and taking her in his arms, kissed her properly for the first time. She responded as his lips caressed her mouth, not caring one iota what the other diners might think.

WHEN THEY RETURNED to the hospital, they peeked into the room before entering. Tessa's mother was watching television, her father was leaning back in the chair with his eyes closed. Jayden was still asleep. Tessa knew her face was flushed and her mother would know exactly what had happened the moment she saw her. After dinner, she and Ben had taken a stroll along the river. She'd never felt so alive nor so much in love. With his arm around her she felt safe and secure, and she knew she would agree to marry him whenever he decided to ask.

Her mother looked up as they entered, her eyes widening before a delighted smile grew on her face. Her father stirred and pulled himself up in the chair. He cleared his throat. "Jayden hasn't woken up," he said, glancing at the bed.

Ben walked to Jayden's side and lifted his hand. Such tenderness and compassion. As Tessa gazed at the man she loved, warmth spread through her body.

"Thank you for staying with him." Ben lifted his head and smiled at her parents.

"Our pleasure." Her mother's eyes had watered. She took a handkerchief out of her bag and dabbed them.

"What are you crying about, love?" Her father placed his arm around her mother's shoulder.

She sniffed and sat straighter. "You need to ask Tessa that."

Her father turned and raised his brow. "Well?"

Tessa slipped her arm around Ben's waist and looked up at him.

He put his arm around her shoulder and pulled her close. "I think your wife has guessed that Tessa and I are now officially a couple."

Her father's brows shot up. "My word, son. Congratulations! When's the date?"

Tessa laughed. "No, Dad. We're not engaged. We're just courting."

"Oh. Well, that's still wonderful. Come here, both of you." He shook Ben's hand and then hugged them both. Her mother gave up dabbing her face and joined in.

A SHORT WHILE LATER, Tessa flew through the front door of her house and nearly stumbled over Sparky. He barked eagerly at her sudden appearance and ran around in circles.

Stephanie called out from the kitchen. "Quiet, Sparky. I'm working on my last case study, and it needs to be good."

Tessa sashayed into the kitchen. "Stephanie! You're not going to believe it." She grabbed her friend's arms and swung her around. "Ben and I are officially courting!"

Stephanie stopped her and held her at arm's length. "It's about time, that's all I can say!"

Tessa laughed. "He asked if he could court me—so old fashioned and proper! And I said *yes*. I can't believe this is actually happening. Pinch me so I know it isn't a dream."

"You're not dreaming." Stephanie smiled as they embraced. "I couldn't be happier for you."

CHAPTER 22

ayden was allowed to go home the next day around noon. He was subdued as he climbed into the seat beside his father. Ben had decided to let a couple of days pass before having a serious talk with him about staying away from Owen and the entire drug overdose situation.

"Are you angry at me?" Jayden asked quietly.

"Angry? No. Disappointed? Yes. But I hope you've learned something worthwhile from this."

"I have." He looked down at his hands. "Never agree to a dare with Owen again."

"Fair enough, but I need to have a serious talk with you about him at some stage. But right now, we have more important things to be concerned about."

"Like what?"

"I need your help in picking out a ring."

Jayden stared at him, eyes wide and mouth gaping. "Have you asked Tessa to marry you?"

Ben's heart fell. He thought Jayden had been warming to Tessa, but his reaction indicated otherwise. Ben shook his head and swallowed his disappointment. "No, but I did ask her to be my girlfriend, and she agreed." When he pulled up at a red light, he turned his head and met Jayden's gaze. "I thought you liked her."

For a long moment Jayden remained silent. "She's all right, I guess." He looked down and fiddled with his hands. "Do you think I'll ever see Mum again?" His voice was quiet and carried a truckload of sadness.

Ben sighed heavily. "I don't know, son. I hope one day she'll come to her senses." He slowed down to take a corner. It was beyond his understanding how Kathryn could be so uncaring about what she'd put Jayden through, but he doubted she'd ever realise the full extent of the hurt she'd caused. He glanced at Jayden and his heart went out to him. *God, please help him get through this.*

After several moments of silence, Jayden lifted his head. "At one of our puppy training classes, Tessa told me her favourite colour was orange. Maybe you could choose a fire opal."

Ben sighed in relief and gave him a broad smile. "Great idea."

THE NEXT FEW days were a flurry of happiness and excitement for Tessa. She was in a constant state of gratitude to God for the goodness He was showing to her and for all the blessings

He was sending her way. And Michael was now just a distant memory in her mind. After waiting and wondering when a good man would come into her life, she could hardly believe she was being courted by the most wonderful man she could ever have dreamed of. Her heart was full of love for Ben, and for Jayden too, though of a different kind.

Whilst she spent as much time with them as she could, she still managed to find time to help Elliott pull off the surprise celebration for their parents' thirtieth wedding anniversary. Hearing about her mother's horrible first marriage had heightened her respect for her parents' long-lasting love.

The day of the anniversary dawned bright and sunny. Tessa joined Elliott on the beach early in the morning. Together, with the help of Stephanie and a few other friends, they ensured the tables and chairs for dining were set up just right. Tall, slender white candles, encircled by pink roses, stood in the centre of each table. Green and white streamers and balloons fluttered overhead in the light breeze. Elliott pointed to a group of people busily setting up a small stage. "See, sis, I hired a live band to play tonight. Nothing too fancy, but they sound swell, so I hope you'll be wearing your dancing shoes."

"I will, and I'm pretty sure I'll have the best partner on the sand," she answered with a wink. Her face lit up as several vans came into view. "Look! The Bussey's crew are here to start the catering."

Elliott laughed. "You really are excited, aren't you?"

"Yes, it's going to be a great night." She turned as Stephanie joined them and slipped her arm around her waist.

"How's the cake coming along, Steph?" Elliott asked.

"Quite nicely. Mum and I finished frosting it late last night.

We were going to make a thirty-layer cake—one layer for each year your parents have been married, but it probably would have been too much."

Elliott nodded. "I think so, but it would've been kinda neat!"

Tessa chuckled. She'd miss her brother when he left to return to the States.

"So now it's just a huge three-layer black forest cake, and on the top is a photo of your parents surrounded by whipped cream and a heart of maraschino cherries."

"I can't wait to see it," Tessa said, giving Stephanie a squeeze. "You and your mother are the best bakers I know."

"Forget about seeing it," Elliott said. "I can't wait to sink my teeth into it."

"Well, you'll just have to hold your sweet tooth until this evening," Stephanie said as she slapped him playfully.

THEIR PARENTS WERE SCRAPBOOKING old photos when Tessa and Elliott dropped by the house later that day. "Do you have any special plans to mark your anniversary?" Tessa asked after she'd hugged and kissed them both.

"Not really. Just being with each other is special enough, but we're going to take a walk along the beach later."

"Maybe have some dinner out," her father added.

Tessa exchanged a glance with Elliott. "What a coincidence," Elliott said. "Tessa and I were just on our way to the beach ourselves. Why don't we go together?"

Their parents agreed, and when they arrived a short while later, they were speechless as family members and friends greeted them with clapping and cheering and happy anniversary wishes.

It was a grand evening of celebration that lasted well into the night. After much of the food was eaten and before the dancing began, Tessa called everyone to attention and launched into the speech she'd prepared. "Mum and Dad, Elliott and I want you both to know how much we love and appreciate you." She paused as her voice caught in her throat. *Don't get emotional now, Tessa...* She swallowed and drew a deep breath before continuing.

"After thirty years of marriage, your love for each other seems to have only grown stronger. We're truly blessed to have such inspiring and godly parents. Thank you for teaching us to be the best we can be. I know I wouldn't be who I am today if it weren't for you two." She paused again and steadied herself. This was much harder than she thought it would be.

She glanced at her notes before continuing. "Your humility, strength, patience, and success push me to be better and to do more each and every day. Growing up, there were so many little things you did for me that I took for granted. I'd now like to say thank you for all those little things, and the big things too, that helped us be the family we are today.

"Dad, thank you for respecting mum and being a man of character and faith. Thank you for your hard work, for teaching me about God, and for always making the best out of life.

"Mum, thank you for your style, your class, and your positive outlook. Thank you for doing my hair every morning before school, for all the wonderful meals you cooked, and for encouraging me to go after my dreams.

"I'm thankful to have been raised by the both of you. The love you have for each other has inspired me to strive for something similar when I get married." She glanced at Ben sitting beside Elliott and Jayden, and her heart warmed. "By example, you've taught me the true meaning of relationships and family. So, from Elliott and me, happy anniversary, Mum and Dad. You deserve this night."

Her father wiped tears from his eyes as he and her mother kissed in front of everyone. Standing, he gazed around at the group of family and friends before settling his gaze on Tessa and Elliott.

Tessa reached for Ben's hand as her father cleared his throat.

"Thank you, Tessa. Thank you, Elliott. You've left me speechless. Your mother and I had no idea you'd organised all of this, as well as the cruise tomorrow, and we're very appreciative of all the effort you've put in. It's been a wonderful night, so thank you." Tears pricked Tessa's eyes when he smiled at her. "I can only say that I hope your Mum and I see many more anniversaries together. And we look forward to seeing what the Lord has in store for the both of you. Although we think we know what, or whom, I should say, He's got in store for you, Tessa." His eyes twinkled as he winked and raised his glass. "We wish you every happiness."

Ben wrapped his arm around her shoulder and popped a kiss on the side of her head as everyone clapped and cheered. They then raised and clinked their glasses with her parents.

EPILOGUE

*T*hree months later, Tessa received a text from Ben asking her to meet him at the park during her lunch break. Nothing unusual about that. They tried to spend as much time together as they could, so after she finished surgery for the morning, she cleaned herself up and headed out.

The park was only a short walk away, and the cooler temperature made walking quite pleasant. She headed for the large Moreton Bay Fig they always sat under, but was surprised to find he hadn't arrived. She checked her watch. Unusual for him to be late.

A dog running towards her in the distance caught her attention. It looked like Sparky, but it couldn't be, Sparky was at home. She looked a little closer. It *was* Sparky, and he was running straight for her with a bow around his neck.

She gave him a cuddle and a pat as he wagged his tail excitedly. "What are you doing here, little man? And what's this?"

She found a small package attached to the bow. The tag said *open me*. "What's going on, Sparky? Who set you up like this?" She looked around, but saw no one. "Guess I'd better open it." She took the ribbon off his neck and opened the package. Inside the wrapping she found a small box. Her eyes widened as she opened it slowly. A beautiful white gold diamond ring sparkled up at her.

"What...?" She looked up as Ben appeared from nowhere and knelt down before her. She felt numb all over. "Ben..." Tears filled her eyes. Her heart thumped as her knees weakened.

He took her hands in his. "Tessa, I'm hopelessly and madly in love with you. I have been for a long time, and I would be the happiest man alive if you agreed to be my wife. Will you marry me?"

"Oh Ben, of course I'll marry you."

Standing, he wrapped his arms around her, lifting her off her feet. As he kissed her, cheers and clapping filled her ears. When she finally managed to extricate herself from his lips, she turned to see who was making the noise. Stephanie stood in front, holding Sparky on a leash, Mum and Dad, with arms wrapped around each other and huge beaming grins on their faces stood to her side, and Jayden stood with Bindy on her other side. No Elliott, but apart from him, the most important people in her world had come to witness this momentous and special occasion.

She gazed into Ben's dreamy eyes and for a long moment thought she was floating. God had given her her heart's desire, and she couldn't be happier. "I love you, Ben." She leaned up and in front of everyone, kissed him slowly and tenderly.

∽

NOTE FROM THE AUTHOR

Hi! It's Juliette here. I hope you've enjoyed the first book in "The True Love Series". Ben and Tessa's story continues in **Book 2, "Tested Love".**

Make sure you're on my readers' email list so you don't miss notifications of my new releases! If you haven't joined yet, you can do so at www.julietteduncan.com/subscribe and you'll also receive a free copy of *"HANK AND SARAH - A LOVE STORY"* as a thank you gift for joining.

Finally, if you enjoyed "Tender Love", help other people find this book by writing a review and telling them why you liked it. Honest reviews of my books help bring them to the attention of other readers just like yourself, and I'd be very grateful if you could spare just five minutes to leave a review (it can be as short as you like).

With gratitude,

Juliette

The True Love Series

Book 2: "Tested Love"

A new marriage, a ready-made family, new challenges and a face from the past all converge to pose the most difficult questions yet for Tessa and Ben. No sooner do they return from their honeymoon in Fiji when Ben's teenage son, Jayden, reverts to old, troubling habits. Ben's parenting style adds to the stress Tessa feels. Part of her wants to coddle Jayden; another part of her wants to support Ben's wishes, but Jayden isn't making it easy for her.

As she frets over marrying Ben and taking on so much responsibility, a new challenge arises. How will Tessa and Ben cope when their worst fear is realized? Will Ben and Tessa have the strength to power through and hold onto God's graces or will the turmoil be enough to make their faith falter? Can this ready-made family remain together, especially now that their worst fear has come to fruition?

The Precious Love Series

Book 1 - Forever Cherished

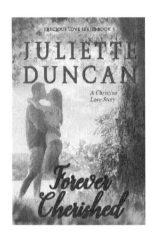

"Forever Cherished" is a stand-alone novel, but is better read as a follow-on from "The True Love Series" books.

Now Tessa's dream of living in the country has been realized, she wants to share her and Ben's blessings with others, but when a sad, lonely woman comes to stay, Tessa starts to think she's bitten off more than she can chew, and has to rely on her faith at every turn.Leah Maloney is carrying a truck-load of disappointments from the past and has almost given up on life. Her older sister arranges for her to spend time at 'Misty Morn', but Leah is suspicious of her sister's motives.

Praise for "Forever Cherished"

"Another amazing story of God's love and the amazing ways he works in our lives. Juliette Duncan writes the best books, everyone of them is worth the read." Ruth H

The Shadows Series

An inspirational romance, a story of passion and love, and of God's inexplicable desire to free people from pasts that haunt them so they can live a life full of His peace, love and forgiveness, regardless of the circumstances. Book 1, *"Lingering Shadows"* is set in England, and follows the story of Lizzy, a headstrong, impulsive young lady from a privileged background, and Daniel, a roguish Irishman who sweeps her off her feet. But can Lizzy leave the shadows of her past behind and give Daniel the love he deserves, and will Daniel find freedom and release in God?

Praise for "The Shadows Series"

"I absolutely LOVE this series. I grew to connect with each of the characters with each passing page. If you are looking for a story with real-life situations & great character development, with the love of God interwoven throughout the pages, I HIGHLY recommend The Shadows Series Box Set by Juliette Duncan!" JLB

"Amazing story, one of the best I have ever read. Gives us so much information regarding alcoholism and abusive behavior. It also gives us

understanding on how to respond. The Bible was well presented to assist with understanding how to accomplish the behaviors necessary to deal with the situations." Jeane M

"This boxed set deeply stirred my soul and thrilled my spirit as God spoke and moved over the despair of alcoholism, Irish tempers, and loss of loved ones." Sharon

Hank and Sarah - A Love Story, *the Prequel to "The Madeleine Richards Series" is a FREE thank you gift for joining my mailing list. You'll also be the first to hear about my next books and get exclusive sneak previews. Get your free copy at www.julietteduncan.com/subscribe*

The Madeleine Richards Series

Although the 3 book series is intended mainly for pre-teen/Middle Grade girls, it's been read and enjoyed by people of all ages. Here's what one 72 year old had to say about it: *I am 72 years of age and thoroughly enjoyed this book. I am looking forward to Book 2 with excitement. Your book can be enjoyed by all ages 11-100. It brings back wonderful memories for the young at heart. Thank you for sharing this book with me. Patricia Walters*

Connect with Juliette:

Email: juliette@julietteduncan.com

Website: www.julietteduncan.com

Facebook: www.facebook.com/JulietteDuncanAuthor

Twitter: https://twitter.com/Juliette_Duncan

98747377R00100

Made in the USA
Columbia, SC
01 July 2018